A PETER OWEN PAPERBACK

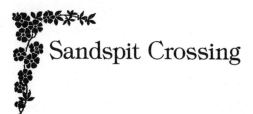 Sandspit Crossing

Noel Virtue

Sandspit
Crossing

PETER OWEN London & Chester Springs

PETER OWEN PUBLISHERS
73 Kenway Road London SW5 0RE
Peter Owen books are distributed in the USA by
Dufour Editions Inc. Chester Springs PA 19425–0449

First published in Great Britain 1993
© Noel Virtue 1993

ISBN 0–7206–0906–2 (cased)
     0–7206–0907–0 (paper)

A catalogue record for this book is available from
the British Library

Printed by Biddles of Guildford and King's Lynn

In memory of the late, great,
once neglected
Ronald Hugh Morrieson,

and for my friend
Mr Berri Groome

Grateful acknowledgement is made to the Queen Elizabeth Arts Council of New Zealand.

A version of the first chapter was published in 1992 by Serpent's Tail, as a short story.

The town of Sandspit Crossing is imaginary, and does not necessarily resemble any New Zealand town – living or dead.

N.V.

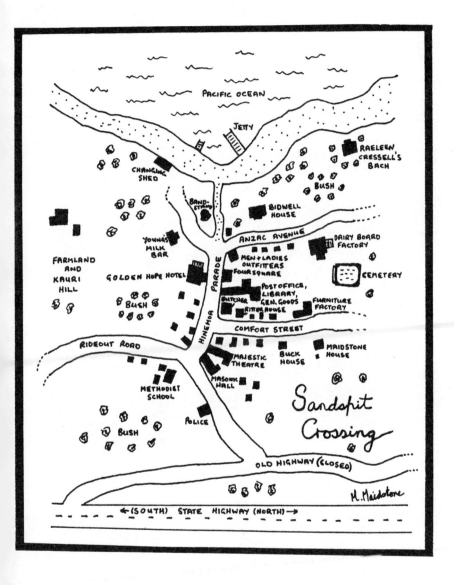

And Along Came a Preacher . . .

Back in the dark ages, when Athol Buck was a sticky-beaked larrikin of thirteen, the Reverend Fulk and his Gospel Crusade of Hope came to town. According to local gossip the country had been swarming with Evangelists and Healers. The war was over. A lot of folk had wanted to get their souls sorted, and to forget the rationing. There was a new age somewhere up ahead.

Athol Buck lived in a clapboard house that his dad Norrie had got built on the cheap and was planning to pay for on the never-never. It even boasted an indoor lavatory. For years Athol's mum Kezia had been living with embarrassment, having to go outside to commune with nature at the old house. That place had been nothing more than a creosoted shack with the outside toilet five hundred yards from the back door and overrun with wetas and spiders and other insects that had no right to live under the wooden seat. It'd been hell in winter.

Kezia Buck loved the new house on Comfort Street. She was the green envy of the neighbours. Though she still harped on about getting more modern all the time. She had been trying for months

11

without success to bag a place on a radio quiz show called *Try Your Luck*. She wanted to have a go at trying to win a brand-new washing-machine, which was the big prize. Despite the fact that two doors along their street the Barkers had bought one and old Granny Barker had trapped both her breasts in the wringer one wash-day and was in hospital for a week.

Sandspit Crossing was an isolated township of jerry-built houses and a main street that led down to a beach few folk ever used. The town was in the far north of the North Island and only a smudge of fly dirt on the map. The main street was called Hinemoa Parade. There was a hotel called the Golden Hope, a Four Square grocery, a Post Office and General Goods where you could buy anything from a pair of black rubber gumboots to a modern bra or health stamps, and a Library. The local flea-pit of a theatre was called the Majestic. Folk would come there from miles around every Saturday night even on horseback, to watch Westerns and James Cagney double bills. The Masonic Hall, a milk bar and a few other places that were either falling down or empty made up the rest of the town's centre. There were a couple of factories. One belonged to the Dairy Board. Athol's dad worked in the other. There wasn't much else. There was no church. Most of the time it was a quiet sort of a place except on Saturday after the hotel was officially closed at six o'clock and drunks wandered all over the main street like Brown's cows, waiting to sneak back in.

Athol's dad was a woodworker. He could do anything with timber. He often cracked on that he had brown fingers, but no one understood what he meant. His jokes usually fell flat. He had got out of going overseas to the war, as some goofy, four-eyed clerk down in Wellington had messed up his papers with someone else's and Norrie was supposed to have been suffering from TB with a spot on his lung the size of a sixpence. He stayed in the country and worked in an office which he'd hated. He and Kezia never did find out what happened to the other bloke. No one told them when the mistake was discovered. The authorities had planned to send Norrie off after that, but for some reason they never got round to it so he said he'd missed the war but the war hadn't missed him. Kezia sometimes half joked that the other poor blighter had probably died a tragic death in Timbuktu so that Norrie might live. It'd been a real miracle. Athol might never have been born, had Norrie been sent away.

Athol was a bit of a Nosy Parker in those days. He wanted to know about everyone and everything. When he saw the posters going up on telegraph-poles around town announcing that the Reverend Fulk was coming, he pestered everyone about who the Reverend was and why he was coming to Sandspit and what he might do if he was out to save people from wicked sin, as it said on the posters. To Athol, wicked sin sounded exciting. He hadn't known much about it at thirteen. A few days later there were even bigger posters put up along Hinemoa Parade. The Reverend Fulk was bringing a complete tribe. There was to be a choir called the Heavenly Hopers, some people called Councillors, two Negro gospel singers from America and a cage of white doves which were to be let loose once the Reverend had finished his soul-gathering. Kezia reckoned it all sounded like a circus was coming to town. There'd not been a real circus in Sandspit Crossing. There had been a half-pie one, Kezia told Athol, years before she had finally married his dad. The township had been a thriving place then. There'd been three clowns, a trapeze artist, two white horses and a geriatric one-humped camel that had belched to music. She couldn't remember what else. Norrie had taken her to have a look but she'd told Athol on the quiet that they'd been too busy getting to know one another carnally and it'd been as rough as guts anyway. She thought the Gospel Crusade of Hope might be almost as good as that circus.

Kezia didn't have much time for Bible-bashing. She thought religion was demeaning to hard-working folk. Yet she and Norrie always laughed a lot about everything and didn't take life too seriously.

Kezia Buck slaved flat stick looking after Norrie and Athol during the years Athol was growing up. She used to make all their clothes. She made all Athol's shirts by hand and knitted socks for Norrie and made Athol's undies out of old sheets that Norrie had ripped with his toenails. Up until Athol was twelve she had run up shorts for him on the Singer out of potato sacks that weren't stained. Then she stopped for some reason and for his thirteenth birthday he'd been given a pair of real serge shorts that had a leather belt with a tin buckle depicting a cowboy riding a bronco.

Because he was a one-off and had no brothers or sisters, Athol spent a lot of time with old folk after school and at weekends. His mum had nagged him into it. There were a lot of old people in Sandspit Crossing. They were those who were also mostly on their own, his mum had explained, and grateful for the company of a thirteen-year-old boy. Athol didn't have any friends his own age. His mum and dad had married late in life and somehow Athol had kept close to them.

His best friend was Miss Magdalen Maidstone. She was in charge of the local Library. Athol didn't like reading much except comics, though he spent a lot of time at the Library. Miss Maidstone had never married. She wore her hair in a tight bun and had a moustache she never shaved off, and despite being somewhere well past forty she was as strong as a Canterbury sheep farmer. Forever baking biscuits when she could get the sugar, making preserves, cooking meat pies when she could afford the meat, she gave her produce away to local folk she reckoned needed a helping hand. Some in town said Miss Maidstone was lonely and needed a good bloke. Athol never had any inkling of her wanting to get married, all the years he knew her.

There was Mr Ritter the butcher. He lived on his own too, behind his shop on the corner of Comfort Street, the same street where Athol lived. Mr Ritter stuffed and mounted dead possums during his spare time in his backyard shed and sold arrangements of them to a shop down in Wellington. He had been an undertaker in Invercargill, but after his wife died from a weak heart he had come north after burying her and given up undertaking. Mr Ritter was the only butcher in town and did a roaring trade in home-made real meat sausages and something called egg stuffing. He stood six feet four inches tall in his socks and was so buck-toothed he could have eaten an apple through a picket fence. He was even more lonely than Miss Maidstone, according to Athol's mum, who'd taken a shine to him years ago. Athol helped Mr Ritter bag up sawdust at the small factory where Norrie worked, carrying the bags back to the butcher's shop, and over the counter Mr Ritter would tell Athol tall stories about pirates and American Indians. He had read a lot of books and been overseas umpteen times. He knew a lot about plays too, and films. Athol hoped that he and Miss Maidstone might get together one day and maybe even get hitched, but Miss Maidstone confessed to Athol when he used to kid her about it that she couldn't stand the man, there was something queer about him, in her opinion, he was a gutless wonder and she reckoned his hair looked like it had been grown on a wild boar's bum.

Miss Maidstone drank whisky when she could get it, wore men's trousers and laughed a lot. She smoked hand-rolled cigarettes and for the last two weeks every April she went off on her Harley-Davidson motor bike to visit her sister Ursula near Dargaville who had once been with a Catholic mission in New Guinea. Athol and Miss Maidstone played footy in her backyard after school, once she'd closed the Library where no one ever went. She loved sport. On Saturday afternoons sometimes in her house the two of them would sit eating home-made popcorn, listening to footy matches on the radio. They'd yell and curse and thump their fists on the table, and some days Miss Maidstone would weep in frustration if her favourite didn't score enough goals. It was the only time during the day when she allowed the radio to be switched on for longer than a few minutes.

Athol used to visit the Bidwell sisters a fair bit. Maudie, Dorothy and Bathsheba Bidwell lived in a ramshackle old house that had once been a farmhouse up until the big Depression of the thirties made changes. They owned five acres of land down near the beach. The land was mostly covered by bush. The week before the Gospel Crusade was due to show up they had a whole acre cleared and laid down with the best sawdust. That was where the marquee was to be erected for the Revival. The Bidwell sisters had been great travellers most of their lives and were very old. They'd lived in Africa, China, England and Rarotonga but had returned to New Zealand and been settled down for years, after Bathsheba broke her pelvis falling off a horse in Dorset and Dorothy had had a nervous breakdown in Bristol. Some said they were rolling in money but no one ever saw any sign of it. The money was said to have been inherited from rich relatives in England who'd died. The sisters were kind and gentle and unworldly. They always gave Athol a good feed whenever he went over to see them after school or sometimes on Saturday mornings if there was nothing worth going to at the pictures. They held church services in their front room on Sundays that no one attended except Miss Maidstone, grew their own vegies and fruit and it was they who had invited the Reverend Fulk to Sandspit. They'd been going on at townsfolk like parrots about their Saviour and that Sandspit was full of sinners ripe for redemption. For weeks before the Crusade they went on so much to Athol about Jesus this and Jesus that, that he started to believe the sisters knew the man personally and that he'd be showing up at the Revival to join in.

Kezia Buck couldn't stand the Bidwell sisters. She'd cross to the other side of the street if she spotted them coming towards her. She thought they were slightly mental and didn't wash often enough. But she never failed to ask Athol in a respectful manner whether or not he'd been over to see how they were getting along. The sisters hoped Athol was going to find the spirit of godly love at the Crusade. As well as his mum and dad and everyone else around town who drew breath. Folk needed it. They'd predicted that Sandspit Crossing was doomed and were trying to prevent a catastrophe.

The township's one claim to national fame was that a legendary sculptress and mystic poet had lived out most of her adult life in a small bach down near the beach, just beyond the town cemetery. Once a year on the anniversary of the sculptress's strange disappearance a long time ago, ten of her female followers from all parts of the country turned up to hold a vigil in the bach. The bach had become a kind of shrine. No one from town was ever asked to attend the annual event, it'd always been carried out secretly. Miss Maidstone had been hankering after an invite for years but hadn't had any luck. The sculptress, whose name was Raeleen Cressell, had lived in poor health and poverty at the bach for decades, back in the 1930s. She'd been such a recluse that local children had been scared to go near the place because adults claimed she wasn't normal and probably a witch. No one had taken much interest in her while she was alive. After Raeleen Cressell disappeared she became famous and folk started turning up from overseas to have a look at where she'd lived. Eventually a plaque was hung above the door of the bach but it was kept locked up as tight as the National Bank on a Sunday by her followers, in between their yearly visits. Few folk in Sandspit were all that interested anyway, even when the ten women turned up in their cars and on motor bikes. One of them would bring a mower and cut the grass, using a scythe when the job got too tough. Trees had been planted all around the property, so it was hidden from sight. No one knew what went on when the vigil took place, though a few reckoned some sort of queer female ritual was held there but had no evidence or proof to back up the claim. A bunch of strange-looking women shutting themselves up in an isolated run-down bach all day once a year was highly suspicious in some folk's minds, yet no one had ever made any effort to find out what they got up to. They were only women after all, as Norrie Buck pointed out to Athol whenever the subject came up, and probably harmless.

The week before the Gospel Crusade was held was also the first week of the school holidays. Athol was taken to school miles away in a run-down old bus. There were only seven children in Sandspit who went out of town to that school, including Athol. There was a kind of a school in Sandspit but it was ruled over by Methodists from Marsden Point, so Athol's mum and dad refused to let him go there as they worried that lessons would be biased. Athol's schoolmate, who went to school on the bus with him, was called Roy Gonda. Roy Gonda's parents were originally from Hungary. He was the same age as Athol but older by a couple of weeks. He grinned a lot. Kezia Buck was never all that friendly to him and Athol reckoned he had so many bad spots that his face was beginning to look like an abandoned quarry, but back then he'd been a mate and couldn't have done wrong in Athol's opinion. Roy Gonda had two hundred butterfly marbles, a real shrunken head from South America that he'd got from a comic advertisement, a twenty-six-inch bike with gears and the biggest Meccano set Athol had ever seen. His mum and dad were well off and owned the local Men and Ladies Outfitters on the corner of Anzac Avenue. They had a modern radiogram in their front room.

Athol's mum didn't like Mr and Mrs Gonda either, because they

were foreigners. She claimed they had more money than most folk
would know what to do with. But she never stopped Athol being
mates with Roy. She thought that as a family the Gondas were far
too toffee-nosed and didn't try to fit into New Zealand ways, but
that they were honest.

Athol saw Roy only during the week and never during the school
hols. Roy was sent down to somewhere just outside Wellington to
stay with his Granny who had a queer name and kept dwarf goats.
She was well off too. Roy let Athol play with his marbles and
sometimes Athol would borrow Roy's bike, as Miss Maidstone was
teaching him how to ride it. For a time, Roy had had his heart's
passion directed at Raewyn Scudder, who was two years older than
him and whose mum had had the largest goitre removed from her
ever heard about in the whole country. One day in the Scudders'
backyard shed Raewyn had let Roy fondle her after she'd made him
wash his hands and she'd pulled down her bloomers. He never
stopped talking about that to Athol. He reckoned he'd got Raewyn
Scudder pregnant because he'd managed to push a wet finger into
her. Athol half believed him for a while because neither of them
knew bugger all about sex.

Norrie Buck spent most of his free time down at the Golden
Hope Hotel after work. It was the only hotel for miles. He drank
there with his mates who were all bludgers, according to Kezia, and
on the make because they'd let themselves go to the pack living in
Sandspit. Norrie shouted his mates drinks and Kezia shouted at him
when he came home so drunk he could barely stand up straight.
He'd lean against the paling fence outside the house and sing dirty
songs at the top of his voice until Kezia went out with a broom and
chased him indoors yelling blue murder, trying not to laugh because
of the neighbours. 'You only think of your belly and what hangs on
the end of it!' she'd yell at him every time he came rolling indoors.
Then she'd start to laugh as soon as the front door was shut.

Yet Norrie treated Athol's mum like she was a queen. He didn't
give a hoot about other women, kept himself clean shaven and
wore a freshly laundered shirt every day. He always made it up to
Kezia after he'd come home drunk and had sobered up. They'd push
off to bed with their arms around each other while Athol was
allowed to stay up and listen to *Night Beat* on the radio, turning the

volume up loud as he liked it and picking fluff off the carpet until
Norrie yelled out to him to knock it on the head and get off to bed
too.

Athol never really found out why his mum hated Bible-bashing.
Kezia had told him and his dad a lot of times over the years that she
believed Bible-bashing was the cause of more family bust-ups than
adultery. It was something to do with her past, the only thing apart
from sex she never talked about. Her family had been Baptists.
There were no photographs in the house of her own mum and dad.
Just her grandad, who'd been part Maori and a hard shot like
Norrie, according to her. Athol overheard her once telling Granny
Barker down the street that her parents had not been all there in
the brains department and that Norrie had saved her skin and
married her before she'd also gone crazy. It was the first and only
time he had heard her speak of her parents, and it hadn't been to
him. Kezia had grown up down in Auckland. She never spoke
about that either. Norrie's past was a mystery. According to him
he'd been dragged up in a children's home, and as far as he knew his
parents could have come down in a flying saucer and left him to be
found under a gooseberry bush.

By the time the marquee had been put up on the Bidwell sisters'
land Norrie and Kezia were fed up to the back teeth hearing about
sinners-who-were-about-to-be-redeemed, so that Norrie was down-
ing Dominion beer as though there'd be no next week and Kezia
was in such a rat-stink mood she was yelling at Norrie twice as
much as she usually did. All Athol cared about at the time was the
excitement in town. Everyone was flapping gums about the Reverend Fulk arriving. The talk built up to fever pitch until all hell
broke loose and life turned sideways.

Athol didn't see the Crusaders arrive. His mum was making up a
new frock that day out of some material Aunt Huldah had sent her.
Athol had to be her model and pincushion. Aunt Huldah was
Kezia's elder sister and ran an old folk's home down in Havelock
North. She was always sending gifts, though they never saw her.
She sent a whole box of French letters once as a joke for Norrie's
birthday and Kezia was livid about that for months. Athol found
out what they were only by stealing one when his mum wasn't

looking and taking it along to show Miss Maidstone, who explained what it was. He thought they were balloons. Kezia claimed everything that Aunt Huldah sent she stole from shops, though she never offered anything to prove the theory.

The Reverend Fulk arrived in a model T Ford painted white with a huge trailer, and the rest of the Crusaders came behind in a green and yellow bus. According to Miss Maidstone, who'd gone along to have a look and later told Athol all about it, the arrival was riveting. She'd even had her hair permed at the beauty parlour so she would look good at the opening meeting of the Revival. She didn't need to find redemption, she was well past that sort of lark, but wild horses couldn't have stopped her from being there to see who did. She even claimed that some bright spark was laying bets as to who might get converted. She was rearing to go when Athol knocked on her door the next morning. Kezia said she didn't mind Athol going to one of the meetings if he was to be in Miss Maidstone's company. But Athol wasn't on any account to go up the front to have hands laid on him or anything else and no one was to force him to either. She and Norrie were having nothing to do with the Revival. Norrie announced that he was taking to the grog in a serious way the whole time the crusading went on. There was a whole pack of his mates planning to whoop it up at the Golden Hope every night, and Kezia cracked on that she might join him, which caused Norrie to develop a hangdog look. He preferred being alone with his mates while he downed the Dominion. Women weren't welcome. He drank Dominion beer by the gallon and swore by it for all sorts of problems.

On the first night of the Revival it seemed like the whole town had showed up. Folk were squashed into the marquee like stunned mullet. It was stifling hot and everyone was wheezing and coughing and sweating. The day had been a scorcher. Miss Maidstone and Athol managed to get a good seat near the front on the side, where she said the Reverend mightn't point. He was well known, she told Athol, for his hell-fire and brimstone preaching, having fits on stage and trying to force the unwary into getting het up and writhing in guilt. The Reverend had been making a real name for himself all over New Zealand. He claimed he could heal the afflicted.

There was a choir at the back of the makeshift stage. They were warming up their voices after Miss Maidstone and Athol had got there and found their way in. A huge sign made of canvas had been put across the middle of Hinemoa Parade. The sign read BE SURE YOUR SINS WILL FIND YOU OUT, and below that was written *Come and Meet Your Jesus Christ.*

Eventually the Reverend came running on to the stage dressed in a white suit and wearing a huge red rose in his lapel and he began shouting straight away, pointing his finger, throwing back his head and jumping up and down while the two Negro gospel singers from America sang so smoothly they kept getting clapped back on stage, and some folk were getting to their feet and shouting hallelujah every five minutes just as they were directed to do in the printed programme and an old boy called Charlie Gregg, who Miss Maidstone claimed was a Commie, fell down and had a fit before he stood up and ran down the front. There were so many went up front when the call came, Athol wanted to hide under the seats. He was scared stiff someone might point the finger at him. But Miss Maidstone held on to him like a vice and whispered in his ear that most of the folk who'd gone up were simply getting a bit carried away with all the excitement. Half of them were boozed to the eyelids anyway, she'd spotted them coming out of the hotel as she and Athol had made their way past it. They were just having a fine time and enjoying every emotional minute.

It was after that first night when strange events started to happen. The first was the Reverend announcing that all the collection money from the last two Revivals he'd undertaken elsewhere in the country had been stolen from the marquee. The news spread over Sandspit like a bush-fire. There was a special meeting called for the afternoon after the money had been discovered missing. It wasn't held in the marquee but right on the main street outside the hotel. Athol ran on down there when one of the neighbours came over to tell Kezia about it. The Reverend was acting quite decent when Athol got there. Surrounded by a few of his cronies he was just talking calmly about thievery in general and at first he wasn't even shouting, but then he suddenly started putting the boot in and acting as if his head was stuffed full of dynamite. There'd been a lot of people gathering nearby. They all listened to what he had to say, but after a bit one of the blokes yelled out for the Reverend to push off and go take a long walk off a short plank. Others joined in and in the end after a lot of shouting back and forth the Reverend said he was sorry for sinners who were deaf and marched off back to where he was staying with the Bidwell sisters. Once he'd gone, folk stood about muttering and whispering amongst themselves. Only one or two in the crowd had stuck up for him.

The next day the big sign that had hung across Hinemoa Parade was taken down and another one put up in its place. The new sign read THOU SHALT NOT STEAL, and underneath had been added *Jesus Is Watching You.*

Norrie came home long after Athol and said there'd been a noisy gathering at the hotel. The police had no clues as to who the culprit was and they reckoned a collection should be organized to replace the Reverend's missing money. Norrie had been all for the idea but the vote they took was ten for to ten against, with some refusing to vote at all, so nothing was done. There were a lot of folk in town who didn't like having religion rammed down their throats and serve the Reverend right for coming to Sandspit in the first place. Yet there were also quite a few who felt sorry for him and had respect for his morals. The Reverend Fulk was only a short little bloke and as pale as a bleached sheet and, as Norrie reckoned, he might be a pimple-head with a mouth on him like a yard of elastic but everyone had a right to a fair go, this was New Zealand.

During the next few days there started to be more thieving and burglary going on all over town than in all Sandspit's history, according to Miss Maidstone. Stores were broken into in the dead of night and goods were taken. Houses were burgled. Someone even stole the light bulbs from all the street-lamps along Hinemoa Parade. And while this was happening the meetings in the marquee became so packed tight full of people that there was a special loudspeaker put up outside so that folk who couldn't get in could sit on the Bidwell property to listen. The Bidwell sisters were rushed off their feet handing out cups of tea and keeping folk off their zinnia beds. People were lining up to use their lavatory as if it was the only toilet in town. And the more successful were the meetings and the more the Reverend got financial from the overflowing collection plates, the more burglaries there were. The Post Office was broken into and hundreds of pounds worth of stamps and ration coupons were stolen. Radios, a refrigerator and a couple of lawn-mowers were stolen from the General Goods. Then folk started stealing groceries from the Four Square while it was still open, getting caught and trying to claim that they'd no idea what they'd been doing and that something queer had come over them. People began to get confused. Some were so upset they were flapping like doors in a hurricane and the police were so overworked they had to send off for help from nearby towns. Within a few days the whole place was going mental. No one had ever seen anything like it. The police were running about like headless chooks, trying to figure out why good honest folk were just helping themselves to anything they fancied. There were a lot who got caught, but the police could do only so much. There were some who got away with it, so it was said. And every night the Revival meetings were packed out. People were coming from as far away as Kaikohe and it was even thought that some of them were joining in the stealing too. It was like a fever had taken over and was affecting folk's brains.

No one Athol knew seemed to be stealing anything. Miss Maidstone told him she would never steal, but she wasn't sure about Charlie Gregg the Commie, as she'd spotted him going about looking dodgy with a crowbar. Windows were broken along Hinemoa Parade night after night until the police put up a huge spotlight and aimed it at all the likely places. But by that time the thefts went on during the day as well and at night most folk were hanging about down at the marquee. The Reverend was raking it in, claiming he'd saved more souls in Sandspit Crossing than he'd saved anywhere else in the whole Northland.

Even Athol's mum got caught up with the fever. She kept searching Athol's room and looking under his bed as if he might be hiding stolen goods there. Norrie was wild at her over that. They had a ding-dong row about it one night in the middle of the backyard with all the neighbours listening in. Kezia had always been as tight as a duck's bum with money and so honest she wrote down everything she bought in a notebook and how much it'd cost so she could show Norrie that she wasn't wasting the housekeeping. She was proud of being honest. She grew so worked up by all the thieving she kept telling Norrie that she believed the Reverend was stirring the pot on purpose and she was certain he had something to do with it. She thought the Reverend acted as mad as the certified anyway and had poisoned minds, or else his cronies had started the thieving themselves and he was covering for them. Norrie yelled at her that she was talking tommy rot, but he didn't know what was causing everything either. No one did.

Folk started buying shot-guns to protect their property after the first few days. Every time Kezia heard a noise out back at night she'd charge through the kitchen to the back door brandishing her broom and yelling out at the top of her voice. She became a nervous wreck. Norrie wouldn't buy a gun. He hated the things and reckoned they would only lead to trouble. Sure enough they did. Mr Ritter caught someone red-handed. The bloke was helping himself to the shop's best meat cuts. He'd broken into the shop through the side-entrance long after midnight. Mr Ritter had heard a noise and taken his new shot-gun out to see what was up and he shot the bugger up the bum, as he put it. And it was one of his regular customers. They took Mr Ritter away but there were no charges laid against him. He didn't even get properly arrested. The next morning there were so many people in the shop congratulating him that Mr Ritter closed early and hid himself away in his house with the blinds pulled down, and he stayed like that most of the time until it was all over. He didn't have any memory of what he had done after the event, he told Athol, his mind had gone blank. The bloke who'd been shot left town and nothing more was said about it. Mr Ritter had used bird slugs, so the burglar hadn't suffered much damage.

The final straw for Kezia was when Norrie turned up one night with one of his hotel mates in an old rust-bucket of a truck. And on the back of the truck for all the world to see was one of the actual models of the washing-machine that Kezia had set her heart on. It was only early evening but Athol was asleep. It was his mum's yelling that woke him up. He looked out of his window and there she was standing on the front lawn with her hands on her hips cursing and swearing at Norrie, and Norrie was standing on the back of the truck leaning over the washing-machine laughing at her. He was as full as a bull he'd been drinking so much. He stood there trying to tell her that the door had been wide open and everyone was helping themselves and why should they lose out? But his words slurred and he didn't make a lot of sense – and as far as Athol knew, there were no washing-machines on sale anywhere in Sandspit, so Norrie must have stolen it from somewhere else.

Well after Kezia shouted at him to take the machine back unless he wanted to lose every organ in his body, she came barging back inside the house still yelling her head off, and she pulled on her gumboots and set out like she had a plague of wasps up her undies. Athol threw on his shorts and a shirt and was off out after her so fast that his dad didn't have time to catch on. Kezia marched along the street in a daze, not looking to her left or right until she was passing Miss Maidstone's gate. And Miss Maidstone must have seen her because she came rushing out and grabbed Kezia by the arm over the fence and nearly caused them both to have a gutzer. They didn't see Athol, as he'd hidden behind a hedge, but they talked for a couple of minutes. Kezia waving her arms about and shouting and then Miss Maidstone rushed out through her gate and marched alongside Kezia swinging her arms, and as they passed under the street-lamps Kezia's face looked like raw liver she was so mad.

Norrie having driven off with the truck before Kezia had even got her gumboots on, Athol followed at a distance. Kezia didn't notice him behind her and Miss Maidstone, or she chose not to. Arm in arm the two headed off and didn't stop until they'd passed all the way down Hinemoa Parade and across Anzac Avenue and had reached the marquee. They barged inside it and went down along the aisle like a pair of tanks. The place was packed to the guy-ropes as it was every night but that didn't faze Kezia. She came to a stop only when she'd reached the foot of the stage, with Miss Maidstone right beside her. The Reverend Fulk was in the middle of shouting the odds on original sin and claiming that the Devil himself was living in Sandspit when Kezia started shouting too and the Reverend came to a dead stop and started down at her with his mouth wide open. Kezia let him have it once she had his attention. She told him straight in front of everyone exactly what she thought of him and his Crusade, shouting that he was a no-hoper and a con-man and a poop-stirrer. Then Miss Maidstone joined in and demanded he leave town straight away. The whole marquee went so quiet you could have heard a mouse blow off. But then a whole group of folk started getting to their feet, clapping and cheering, and then Kezia and Miss Maidstone clambered up on to the stage and the Reverend backed off, calling out 'Now ladies, now ladies!' No one took a blind bit of notice, the clapping just grew louder.

Well, whatever else Kezia shouted (Athol couldn't hear everything from where he stood at the back), she stirred up a lot of other women. They started following her up on to the stage. There were shaking fists and shouting voices and the Reverend backed away holding up his arms trying to protect his head from bashing handbags, and the choir of Heavenly Hopers, who'd still carried on singing in low voices, stopped singing and started to push forward *en masse*. In a minute there were so many women on-stage that Athol lost sight of his mum just as he saw her raise her fist to sock the Reverend on the jaw.

Then suddenly there was a screeching, wrenching sound. The whole stage began to collapse inward and all the women and a couple of blokes who'd joined them were screaming their heads off and flaying about. Soon there were bodies all over the show lying struggling on top of each other. Women who hadn't managed to get up on to the stage leapt back in sheer panic. Athol tried to shove his way down to the front but didn't get far. Suddenly everyone was trying to leave. He eventually got knocked over because he was only small, but he managed to roll himself into a ball, covering his head and hoping for the best. He got walloped across the back by boots and shoes, and the noise was loud enough to bust ear-drums.

Kezia suffered a broken wrist, two cracked ribs and got a black eye. Miss Maidstone had her left leg fractured and someone ripped her frock open down the back, and whoever it was also stole her bra, so she later claimed. Quite a few got badly hurt. Someone telephoned for a couple of ambulances, which took two hours to arrive. Folk lay about moaning and crying and some of the women were dragged across into the Bidwell sisters' house to wait for the ambulances. It was like the aftermath of a battle. The nearest hospital was fifteen miles away and Athol went with Kezia and Miss Maidstone and a lot of others on the back of a truck, as the ambulances were full.

After her wrist was set and her chest was taped up and they'd set and plastered Miss Maidstone's leg, Kezia demanded they be taken back home. She wasn't going to stay the night in hospital, miles away from Norrie. She was still in such a bad temper the hospital authorities agreed and the three of them got back home in the early hours of the next morning. Kezia asked Athol to make a bed on the settee for Miss Maidstone. Both she and Miss Maidstone slept the clock round.

By lunch-time the next day the marquee had been pulled down and the Reverend Fulk and his cronies had done a bunk without anyone really noticing. The Bidwell sisters also left town that same day, without saying goodbye to anyone and not even leaving a note. A few weeks later their house was put up for sale.

It was thought by half the town that Kezia Buck had been right to do what she'd done, that it had been the Reverend all along who had stirred everything up, that he'd been in on the thieving somehow but no one could figure out how or why. There seemed no earthly or heavenly reason for it. The thieving and the burglaries stopped as soon as the Reverend went. The Reverend Fulk was supposed to be a respected gospel preacher and had made a lot of people religiously happy all over the north, according to gossip. There was much confusion in the days following. Some folk reckoned the thieving might have been caused by something in the water. The town supply was tested, but that was all right. Foodstuffs from the Four Square were taken away to be looked at, but there wasn't one clue as to why the town had gone haywire.

A week or so later, out of the blue, a letter and cheque arrived, care of Mrs Gipson who ran the Post Office. The cheque was for hundreds of pounds and the letter was from the Reverend Fulk. In the letter he claimed that he didn't know what had happened either and believed most sincerely that it had been the Devil himself at work. Satan the Beast lived in Sandspit Crossing, he was certain of it, and he had followers all over the place. One of the Devil's cohorts probably lived in Sandspit too, and had helped destroy what he was trying to achieve for the country. The money was to compensate for the damage done, and to apologize for the whole terrible affair. Well, that news flew all over the place like an old man's spit. Folk in town were stumped. It was the last thing anyone had been expecting.

Life settled down again eventually. Two years later Roy Gonda ran
off and joined a freight-ship after it was announced that Raewyn
Scudder was pregnant. That caused a lot of ear-wagging for a few
weeks. The Bidwell sisters' house remained empty and boarded up.
No one bought it. Miss Maidstone kept on opening the Library
every day and sitting in there with no customers except Athol,
despite her new reputation. They would sit there together after
school surrounded by books, and she taught Athol how to play
poker and gin rummy. She nagged him about heading off to find a
nice clean girl-friend. Some days she read aloud from Shakespeare
or Dylan Thomas.

Athol's mum finally got herself on to the radio quiz show *Try
Your Luck*. They asked her to appear on the very last show because
she had written more letters to try to get on it than anyone else had
in the whole of New Zealand. She never did win the washing-
machine. In fact she won nothing at all. But when she arrived
home on the coach from Wellington, Norrie and Athol were
waiting for her at the bus station in Kaikohe with the news that
Norrie had been saving up for a machine on the quiet and one was
to be delivered the very next day. After she clambered down off the
coach dressed like a dog's dinner with her hair all over and looking
irritated as it was raining, her eyes grew as huge as globes when
Norrie told her what he'd done. She was speechless. There were
still only a few families in town who had been able to afford a
washing-machine.

That same week Kezia started washing clothes for some of the
neighbours on Comfort Street and kept it up for a long time until
people were able to buy one themselves on time payment. She
never charged them a penny either, which Norrie reckoned was a
bit lamb-brained but Kezia was a good sport. People wouldn't let
her forget about the night she and Miss Maidstone faced the
Reverend Fulk and sorted out the town by doing so. Somehow the
Reverend copped all the blame anyway whenever anyone brought
the subject up and went on about past days. There were plenty of
rumours about him afterwards, that he was a shyster, a liar and a
well-known cheat. Athol's mum and Miss Maidstone became a
couple of heroines in a few folk's eyes. Mr Ritter proposed marriage
to Miss Maidstone a few days later but she turned him down. The

Reverend went down in the town's history as a rum bugger. No one heard anything more about him. He just disappeared off the face of the world, as far as Sandspit was concerned.

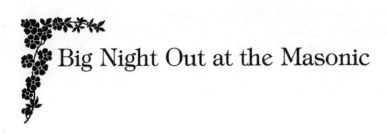

Big Night Out at the Masonic

A short while before a play called *Private Lives* was put on at the Masonic Hall, Miss Maidstone found the bloated corpse of Dan McCauley washed up on the beach. She'd been down there for her usual morning ramble at dawn that morning and told Athol later that at first sight she'd thought the near-naked corpse was a stranded whale. Dan McCauley had been a big bloke.

Athol had turned fifteen by then and had finished with school. Roy Gonda had already run away to sea on the freighter and folk had stopped thinking that Raewyn Scudder was pregnant by him, but it was about the same time when the news flew around that her mum had been lying about it anyway. No one talked about the Reverend Fulk any longer. That was long-dead history. Dan McCauley's death dominated the tongue-wagging for days. It turned out that he had drowned himself. He had left notes saying that he was going to do it stuffed inside letter-boxes all over town. He claimed in the notes that his wife had nagged him every minute of the day for twenty-five years and he'd had more than a gutsful of her and of life in general. As Norrie kept asking at the time, why hadn't he just packed up and shipped out across the ditch to Australia instead of doing the ultimate dirty on himself? It was highly suspicious. A lot of folk felt that way. The poor beggar would be a long time staring at the lid. It was said that he'd been hanging about the hotel as mopy as a wet hen for weeks, drinking like a fish, prior to joining marineland.

Mrs Kathleen McCauley, Dan's wife, had always been thought of as a bit of a gutsache even by the kindest tongues in town. It was said that if she had ever laughed, her face might've developed cracks as wide as those in parched summer earth. But no one blamed her for her old man's suicide. It was put down to his having lost whatever good judgement he might have possessed in life. She got a lot of sympathy about it when she was out and about Hinemoa Parade after the funeral was over and Mr McCauley was tucked up in his plot over at the cemetery.

The State having finished trying to educate Athol Buck, he'd been helping out Mr Ritter in the butcher's shop, while Miss Maidstone was setting up the plan she had of officially employing him as an Assistant Librarian. She had been granted permission to employ him but was waiting for papers to be signed by some Government clerk down in Wellington who she said needed a good kick up the bum to get his fingers moving. It had something to do with Athol's not being qualified for the job. As it happened, the day before Dan McCauley's corpse was discovered by Miss Maidstone, Mrs Kathleen McCauley had been in the butcher's when Athol was there working. She'd been arguing with Mr Ritter over the sale of some best beef Athol had delivered, which, she claimed, ponged to high heaven and was close to being maggoty. She caused a ruckus, having barged in waving the piece of beef in the air, and in a real foul temper pushed Mrs Dolly McArthur, who suffered from flatulence and the occasional migraine, into the front of the fake marble counter. Mrs McArthur protested that Mrs McCauley had jumped the queue and was so upset at being shoved aside she let out the loudest fart anyone could expect from a human being. A lot of others there couldn't help laughing. But Mr Ritter didn't laugh. He didn't even smile. He took one look at Mrs McArthur's bright-red face and puckered lips and said to her in a comforting voice: 'Don't you fret. Don't take a blind bit of notice, Mrs McArthur. It's a sad arse that can't rejoice.'

Norrie Buck told Athol that *he'd* never felt any compassion for Mrs McCauley or her old man. He reckoned they'd both been openly bludging off the Social Security scheme since it had begun way back in 1938, furnishing their whole house and even buying a second-hand baby Austin with all the handouts.

Miss Maidstone was possibly the only person in Sandspit Crossing who ever went down to the beach, except Athol. It was a desolate place even in the height of summer and thought to be smelly enough to make the most stout-hearted person heave up breakfast. The beach was situated at the far end of Hinemoa Parade, where a dirt-track leading through gorse bush passed alongside the Bidwell sisters' land, which was still fenced off and abandoned two years after they'd gone away. There were a couple of run-down and rotting jetties on the beach. Further along was an old changing shed where the half-eaten carcases of three sheep had once been discovered. If anyone wanted a safe swim they usually went further north to somewhere like Opononi, as Sandspit beach had a bad undertow. Norrie, Kezia and Athol had taken Miss Maidstone up to Opononi one Boxing Day after the last war had ended but Norrie's van, which he'd since sold for scrap, broke down at Mamaranui and Kezia was sick all over the back seat, so they'd turned back after the van had been fixed.

Just at the end of Hinemoa Parade was Young's Milk Bar and Grill. Athol went there quite often. The owners, Jack and Beryl Lamb, made the tastiest toasted sandwiches in the north when the fillings were available, and sometimes Miss Maidstone took Athol along there for a shout and bought a couple of cheese-and-apple toasties and two banana-flavoured milk shakes before they sat out on the grass verge watching the world go by. Not that much of it ever did. The new State Highway had seen to that, cutting Sandspit off so that anyone driving north could bypass the town completely. There was a lot of talk about places that might be closing down and folk who were planning to move away by the time Athol had turned fifteen. Kezia herself was dead set on herself, Norrie and Athol selling up and heading south to start again where the money was, but Norrie was happy enough to stay put and see what happened. It was a worrying time for Kezia and Norrie. Money was short, they argued about the lack of it more and more often and Norrie got drunk almost every night and sometimes on Sunday he was blotto the whole day. The two years since Athol became thirteen had seen a lot of changes.

When the news broke that there was going to be a real live play put on at the Masonic Hall, a few folk became a little giddy and then stories about it grew and were stretched a mile. Folk started telling each other that a couple of famous film stars from Hollywood in America were possibly coming to act in the play, which excited Kezia, but in the end it was only some New Zealand-run outfit called the Community Arts Service. It was Dolly McArthur who put it about that Rita Hayworth and Bob Hope, who were touring Australia, were coming. She told everyone that they were being flown into town in a Government-owned helicopter and for a while some started to believe the rumour because they wanted to and flapped about where the helicopter might possibly set itself down and who would be on the welcoming committee. There was no airstrip handy – no one being aware that a helicopter didn't need an airstrip. Kezia told Athol that on one of the outlying farms there'd once been an attempt at establishing a sort of flying club. Norrie had been involved with that. He and one of his best drinking mates from the hotel had built a home-made Tiger Moth from plans that had been handed down from someone else's grandfather. They'd built the body of the plane out of handouts and were still hunting for the engine parts when one night Norrie left the plane sitting out in a paddock and cows had chewed their way through the sago-coated wings.

The rumours about the play and who was to be in it were pushed around from one set of lips to another until Miss Maidstone as Chief Librarian got an official letter from the Arts Service as well as a handful of public notices regarding the play, which Athol helped her nail up in shop doorways. *Private Lives* by Noël Coward was to be put on at the Masonic for one night only and tickets were to be sold so that only those who bought them could attend the performance. It certainly wasn't going to be a free night out. The hall held only about a hundred people and that'd be a squeeze, and after the notices went up the tickets began to get sold like hot pikelets. Everyone in town and for miles around wanted to go, most never having heard of Noël Coward or seen a real play in their lives before. It was to be a hugely special occasion, for apart from the picture shows at the Majestic, there was usually nothing at all going on in Sandspit to make anyone think they were on a good trot living there. As Miss Maidstone often cracked on, anyone who suggested a bet on two flies crawling across the hotel ceiling on a Saturday night would be likely to draw a crowd. So expectation about the play grew quickly. It was something to relieve the monotony. Even after the notices announcing who was to be in it had been read, a few folk still clung on to the idea that someone famous might show up to get an oar in on the proceedings. No one had heard of the actors who were coming. They were nobodies from Wellington. One of them had acted in Australia.

It was Mr Ritter who had cottoned on to the idea. He claimed he had written to someone he knew down in Wellington asking if the Arts Service, which he'd read about in *The Weekly News*, would consider travelling as far north as Sandspit. He'd had an idea, he told Athol one morning, that it would be just the job. It might pull folk together, what with all the fretting about whether or not Sandspit Crossing was going to survive because of the State Highway. The Highway was buggering up business. It'd been a year since the motor camp behind the Dairy Board factory had closed down. The beach had been left to rack and ruin, and was now strewn with rotting seaweed and dead fish that hadn't been cleared away and invaded by so many blowflies and midges that if anyone did go along there on a summer afternoon with their mouth open they were more than likely to choke to death. Without holiday folk turning up with money to burn and with locals so uneasy and planning to shut down and abandon Sandspit, the threat to the town's future was shaky, to say the least. Mr Ritter reckoned he'd been warning folk for a long time about what could happen. The Dairy Board were threatening to shut their factory one day and move it further south. Half the township worked there. It was a crying shame. There sure wasn't much attraction for anyone to come to Sandspit Crossing. Even the local farmers were starting to go elsewhere. No entertainment except for the Picture Theatre, and if anyone was foolish enough to go there for a night out they'd spend the next two weeks counting the number of fleas that would jump on to them from the horsehair seats.

Miss Maidstone, who thought the advent of the play was the most exciting thing to have happened since outbreaks of war, had been trying hard to get Athol interested in culture for some time. Advancing him away from reading *Dan Dare* and *Phantom* comics, she'd introduced him to *Classics Illustrated* instead, hoping that he would move along from those to reading books. With stars in her eyes and hope in her heart she came up with the idea to make a big poster about the play with a headline that read *A Little Bit of Culture Does You Good*. Mr Ritter turned out to be so taken with the idea when Athol told him about it that he paid out of his own savings to have such a sign made and hung over Hinemoa Parade, similar to the signs the Reverend Fulk had brought with his Gospel Crusade. Days before the acting troupe and the van full of scenery and coloured lights were to arrive, three days later than was originally planned, the sign, made of canvas with huge red letters, was hoisted up with ropes across Hinemoa Parade between the hotel and the Four Square grocery. But for some reason whoever it was who painted the sign had got muddled and the sign ended up as *A Little Bit of Couture Does You Good*, which a lot of folk didn't understand and, even if they had, couldn't have acted on it as the Men and Ladies Outfitters previously owned by the Gondas, who'd left town heading for Wellington, had gone out of business. No one bothered to change the wording. It didn't seem to matter. Everyone knew the proper expression off by heart anyway after Miss Maidstone had told everyone it was her idea and had bandied the words about by the time the big night was just around the corner. *Private Lives* was about to take over and, after it had been performed, the arty folk from Wellington would be off out of town as fast as a bride would throw off her nightie.

Meanwhile, without Athol's knowing it, Miss Maidstone had received the signed papers from Wellington telling her that Athol was allowed to be her Assistant at the Library, with a view to his taking over one day when she did retire. The job of Librarian was worth only a few pounds a week, but someone had decided that the Library must be kept open. The first Athol knew about his new job was when he read about it on printed handbills that Miss Maidstone had made up on an old Gestetner machine in the back room of the Library. She told Athol she'd come up with the idea for the handbills the same time as she'd found inspiration for the play poster and had gone ahead to give him a surprise. Late one night after the Buck household was asleep, she'd hiked all over town tacking up the handbills on every wooden telegraph-pole she could find in the dark and shoving the rest into letter-boxes, The hand-bills read *Athol Buck to Be Future Librarian. Local Boy Makes Good.* Each one went on to also announce Miss Maidstone's planned retirement and that she would like a party to be held in her honour if folk could come up with some cash and a bit of time.

That news didn't cause even a ripple, most folk finding the subject of the local Library to be as about as exciting as a leaky pipe. A lot of folk even got riled because Miss Maidstone was wasting valuable paper when there were still shortages. And most already knew that Athol would probably end up working in the Library because Miss Maidstone and he were mates. No one else would want the job. A few wondered why the town Librarian had decided to retire when she was still capable of sitting in there all day. It didn't require much effort for the job.

Kezia was as proud as a peacock about Athol's new status. She told Athol she'd got tickets for the big night at the Masonic so they could all go together just to celebrate, and afterwards they could hurry on down to Young's Milk Bar and Grill before it shut and have a supper of flounder and chips. She'd got it all worked out. She even went round to see Mr Ritter at his house after he'd shut up shop to tell him that her son would be leaving his employ now he had a proper Government job that was worthy of his talents. And she bought Athol a brand-new fountain-pen and a bottle of ink out of her housekeeping money. She told him he'd need it but not to let on to Norrie, who would blow his stack because he hated the whole idea of his only son becoming a librarian. According to her, Norrie had been knocking Miss Maidstone's plan since he'd first heard of it, as he reckoned libraries were for sissies. 'You can't make honey out of dog-shit,' he told Kezia every time the subject came up. Kezia told Athol that he'd said it so many times like a stuck record she'd have knocked him into the middle of next week if Athol hadn't been offered the job. She'd known in her heart for years that Athol would go a long way in life.

Athol hadn't enjoyed working for Mr Ritter. The man had some queer ideas. He'd constantly sent Athol out back to his house to fetch things. Athol had hated that. There was an atmosphere inside the house of something having died there. Mr Ritter explained that it was the chemicals he used for curing and stuffing the dead possums he sold to the shop in Wellington. He claimed he had stuffed hundreds of dead possums over the years as well as a few magpies and it brought him a little extra money. He tried to get Athol interested in stuffing possums but Athol would have nothing to do with the pastime. The rooms of Mr Ritter's house were filthy. They'd begun to smell like the back end of a brewery horse. Athol secretly reckoned the man was not quite right in the head. And butchers might be needed in society, Miss Maidstone had one day confessed to Athol, but being one made Athol's clothes smell so bad that after he'd nicked over to see her after work she wanted to have her house fumigated. She never knew why New Zealanders wanted to eat so much meat: it ruined the blood, played hell with a healthy digestion, and made women as aggressive as men.

Mr Ritter had some secret plans in his house, drawn on blue paper and pinned to the walls of his living-room as well as spread out on a chrome-legged table. He pointed them out to Athol one day and made him swear never to tell anyone about them, so Athol didn't. The plans were for a kind of church which Mr Ritter had dreamed about building for years. He'd even picked out a site where the church could be constructed, down near the old abandoned changing shed on the beach, where it would be seen for miles even by sailors in passing ships. He had a soft spot for sailors, he admitted, as his father had been one. He had an idea for a flashing neon sign to be attached to the front of the church as well, for night-time advertising. It wasn't to be an ordinary church but one for men only, to get away from their wives or their sweethearts because all men needed to do that from time to time. The church was to be called the Chapel of Enduring Masculinity.

Athol didn't understand the name and he still didn't really understand what it meant after Mr Ritter had done his best to explain. There were to be no windows, so women passing by could not peer in, there'd be a hotel-type bar selling whisky and beer, which was all real men should drink, a luxury pool-table room, a room for secret initiation ceremonies and another back room where blokes could strip naked and wrestle. The main area of the church would look like any other church, with pews and a pulpit and a large organ. Mr Ritter planned to be the preacher. He'd written a lot of down-to-earth talks that he hoped to give on Saturday nights. The whole idea was to do with New Zealand blokes needing to rediscover their threatened maleness which had been at a low ebb since the war ended. He'd also recently come up with the idea of building a small bath underneath the pulpit which could be opened up and used as a baptismal so that men could be baptized back into being aware of where they really were in life, to understand their place in the scheme of things which had gone too far away from basics.

None of it made a blind bit of sense to Athol. He never let on. A lot of what Mr Ritter said about the church when he and Athol were alone made Athol a bit uneasy. Once Mr Ritter had shown him the plans he wouldn't stop talking about the church for days at every opportunity. Some of what he said even sounded dirty. Mr Ritter told him one morning that the penis was the most misunderstood organ in the male body and he had a vision, a mission to help blokes understand it, and why it had been provided. They'd lost touch with it, what it meant to have been blessed with a penis, however small or large it turned out to be. Women over the years had caused it to shrivel, and he had ways and means of helping to make every New Zealand penis larger. Athol kept half expecting Mr Ritter to take his own penis out to demonstrate, the way he went on. 'There's more to the penis than meets the eye, son,' he would state to Athol when they were alone in the shop.

Yet Mr Reginald Wallace Ritter was the town butcher and no one disliked him or found him odd, as far as Athol could tell. He was well thought of in town and was very kind when Kezia told him that Athol was going to work in the Library. He presented Kezia with a bunch of wild freesias, a dozen home-made sausages and three beefsteaks, and gave Athol a silver-plated pocket-watch that had belonged to his grandfather. Kezia tried to make him take the pocket-watch back but Mr Ritter wouldn't hear of it. He confessed to Kezia that he felt proud having had her handsome son working for him at the shop, because he believed that one day Athol was headed for fame and fortune and he wanted a part in helping that to happen. When Kezia told Norrie what Mr Ritter had done, Norrie said New Zealand was full of all sorts, whatever blew your dress up, Mr Ritter was a butcher and that was a respectable way of making a living if you were a normal bloke. Athol should have stuck with it instead of having namby-pamby ideas about books.

It didn't stop raining for days before the night of the play. It was midwinter with muddy days that were short and cold, and folk were feeling down-hearted because the main street had flooded, through the drains being blocked. A lot of the rain had mixed with escaped sewer water and it had poured into shop-fronts and into the hotel. Sandspit was beginning to look and smell worse than it sometimes did in the middle of summer when there was a drought.

Kezia had been going on at Norrie about their moving away. She'd heard there were well-paid jobs growing on trees down in Wellington, and if they moved there she could find a job as well and they'd be landing on their bums in butter instead of just sitting on them in Sandspit worrying and arguing about money. Since Athol had now left school and had all the education he'd been able to grab hold of, he could go with them if he wanted to. He was old enough now to make up his own mind. Though Athol had more chances of finding a decent wife down south, even if they had to move to the city to do it. Athol might be only fifteen but his adult life was just up around the corner. Kezia hadn't nagged Norrie so much for years. Norrie didn't know how to handle it. He was off down at the hotel with his mates every hour he could find after work, which just made Kezia lam into him all the more when he was home. Athol started to spend more and more time across at Miss Maidstone's house.

Though Miss Maidstone lived next door to the Bucks, there were a couple of empty sections between her place and theirs, and an area of gorse bush. Her house was set well back off Comfort Street facing north, just the way she liked it. She hated noise. There was a small radio in her living-room and a piano that had seen better days, but there was no gramophone and she liked the radio to be switched on only after dark, except when she listened to Rugby matches on Saturday afternoons. She explained to Athol that listening to the radio in the daytime was just an excuse to be a member of the Slackarse Club and most of what came over the air-waves just went in one ear and out the other and addled the brain. Folk should be forced to wake up to that fact or else they might find themselves laughing on the wrong side of their faces or dead without having achieved anything in life. Being lazy was the worst sin Miss Maidstone knew of, she told Athol. She talked to him non-stop, while he was with her.

Miss Maidstone's house was mostly quiet and peaceful, filled with old books piled up on rickety wooden shelves that she'd made herself out of orange-boxes. There were bookshelves in every room, and on every wall, held there with dressmaking pins, were dozens of souvenirs from all over New Zealand. She had travelled to every corner of the country on her Harley-Davidson motor bike years ago and was often planning new trips. She spent hours sitting at her formica-topped table in the kitchen writing letters and cards to people she had met on her travels. She posted cards for their birthdays and cards for Christmas, there were special cards at Easter and sometimes she parcelled up books that she'd removed from the Library shelves when she considered them to be worn out. Yet she almost never received any mail in return. No one ever showed up to visit her. Athol had asked her once why all those folk who were supposed to be friends never bothered with her. Miss Maidstone just laughed and said they were far too busy to bother with the likes of her, but she wrote to them anyway as she believed they enjoyed hearing all her news. One day she might be rewarded for all her efforts.

Athol enjoyed listening to her talk. She had a lot to say. Norrie often called her Motor-Mouth behind her back, but he liked her as much as Athol and Kezia did, along with half the town. She was Miss Magdalen Maidstone, the brainy old bird of Number 13 Comfort Street, and if anyone ever did find the need for a book, or some advice from a book, they knew where to go to find it. She never thought of herself as being lonely, as Athol secretly feared she was. Her constant talking kept loneliness at bay, she told him. And down at the back of her section, in her outside lavatory which was painted sky-blue inside and out, she kept a brand-new roll of the best toilet-paper wrapped up in a pink linen bag, just in case, she'd explained to Athol, one day she might receive a visit from one of the dozens of folk all over the country to whom she exposed her heart.

Rain stopped falling three hours before *Private Lives* was due to get started. Miss Maidstone, Kezia and Athol were outside the Masonic Hall a full hour beforehand, as Norrie had decided he couldn't face it and Kezia wanted to try to sell his ticket to someone else. Both she and Miss Maidstone and every woman in town were dressed up to kill that night. They'd all had their hair done and had trowelled the make-up on, and the air outside the hall was so full of Evening in Paris that a lot of men tried not to gag as they waited to be allowed in. Folk with tickets were supposed to queue up outside. Family groups stood about calling to each other and the general excitement got too much for a while when a couple of elderly ladies from Mount Wesley fainted and were laid out on the grass verge until they'd recovered. Children were racing about all over the pavement dressed in their Sunday best screaming their heads off and the Majestic Picture Theatre decided to close down for the night as it hadn't managed to get in anyone at all to see a rerun of *Snow White and the Seven Dwarfs* which had packed folk into the aisles when it had been shown the week before.

There were no reserved seats. No one wanted to buy Kezia's spare ticket when she offered it around. It was everyone for themselves when the doors were finally opened. There was a real stampede. Miss Maidstone hung on to one of Athol's arms and Kezia hung on to the other and they shoved and pushed along with everyone else to get in and pelted down the centre aisle as fast as they could to get down near the front. People were laughing and yelling out cracks and it was happy bedlam-time for a while until all the seats were taken. But something must have gone wrong because there were dozens more ticket-holders than there were seats and folk kept pouring into the hall in ever-increasing waves, finding places to sit on the floor below the stage and at the side or hanging on to the wooden struts down the side-walls until all sorts were being packed in so tightly together that many were pushed out through the open side-doors before they realized what was going on, and had to run all the way round to the front to get back inside again, still laughing and joking. Carloads of people hauling trailers filled with giggling children were turning up from all over the north.

Not that many out-of-towners had bothered to dress up for the occasion. There were farmers in black singlets and shorts still wearing gumboots as if they'd just come in from scattering silage, blokes in old paint-stained boiler suits who'd decided to show up at the last minute, and more than half the crowd had failed to buy tickets, though in the end no one was turned away. There were hordes of children in bare feet and babies carried across shoulders and eventually someone herded all the older children down to the front and made the adults already sitting there on the floor move back to squash themselves into aisles that were already bursting. The walls were bulging and it was almost an hour before everyone started to quieten down and the doors were shut. The Arts Service had managed to hang curtains across the front of the stage. When the lights suddenly went out, a few spotlights hanging from ropes tied to the ceiling rafters came on. Everyone oohed and aahed as the spotlights were red and blue in colour and the atmosphere added to the tension.

When a well-dressed man appeared through the gap in the curtains wearing a dinner-suit and a bow-tie, a group of young blokes standing down the front started catcalling and whistling at him until some of the older folk yelled out at them to pipe down. The man waited with upraised arms and a sickly grin on his face until it was almost completely silent in the hall and in a fruity voice began to give a talk about the Theatre, explaining who Noël Coward was and why plays like *Private Lives* were to be enjoyed by everyone. Few folk took in what he said. Many hadn't seen each other for months and were catching up on news over the heads of others, babies had started screeching and some of the smaller children up at the front were beginning to giggle and wrestle with each other out of boredom. There were quite a few calling out from the back that they couldn't hear a thing and to get on with it as they'd never get it over with before the hotel was officially shut for the night. Miss Maidstone kept squirming in her seat. She kept turning round to glare at people sitting behind her. She'd taken off her straw hat and had almost crushed it to pieces in her hands. To the hat she'd pinned a dozen Wellington souvenirs.

Eventually the play got going. Athol, Kezia and Miss Maidstone had seats on a wooden form that wobbled, four rows from the front. When the man withdrew and the curtains opened, everyone in the audience started talking out loud about the scenery, so the first few lines from the actors were lost. Miss Maidstone sat leaning forward trying to hear, holding on to Athol's hand, having let her hat drop to the floor. She acted enthralled. Most of the audience soon tried their best to follow the story-line too, but some folk kept laughing out loud sometimes for no reason at all. They thought they were supposed to, as it was a comedy they were watching. When one of the actors stepped up to the front of the stage and started pointing towards the back of the hall and talking about some ship he could see, quite a few people stood to their feet to have a look as well, encouraging most of the smallest children down front to scramble across each other to the aisles trying to peer back at what they thought must be going on that they didn't want to miss. When a character called Amanda went to light up a real cigarette a couple of young blokes who were leaning against the front of the stage clambered up on to it and offered to light it for her and almost knocked her over in their rush. The actress was very polite and just smiled. After letting one of them light the cigarette she whispered something and they quickly jumped down off the stage, red-faced, with wolf-whistles coming from the envious.

Most of the men in the audience had bottles of beer they were drinking from and many families had bought sandwiches wrapped in newspaper. A few families had brought fish and chips. Half-way through the first act someone came in with a tray of ice-blocks, which created a rush. It all moved along and people got caught up in the action and in the second act when there was a terrific fight on-stage between the lead characters, lamps and cushions were thrown about and furniture was tipped over and there was a great deal of shouting and arguing. Even the children sitting up at the front went quiet while that was going on, but quite a few adults started shouting out and a woman called Mrs Ida Grey sitting next to Kezia who sometimes worked part-time at the Milk Bar and had had a pig of a husband stood to her feet and shouted at the top of her voice: 'You should be really ashamed of yourselves!' and started to cry. Kezia reached up and gently pulled her back down, whispering to her that it was just part of the story, it wasn't real, it was play-acting. Mrs Ida Grey was very het up but then she did calm down and loudly whispered to everyone around her that she'd got a bit unnerved, it reminded her of the fights she'd had at home with her husband Cyril before he died, though they didn't have as nice a living-room and Cyril had belted her over the head with a rolled-up newspaper before passing out. Everyone was so concerned for her that the play stopped for a while until Mrs Grey had pulled herself together and blown her nose a few times with Athol's handkerchief.

In the interval that followed the fight another woman who lived in Comfort Street called Mrs Enid Mills, who was known as the most house-proud person in Sandspit, quietly made her way down to the front, hoisted up her frock, climbed up on to the stage and started to tidy everything up, as the curtains had been left open. A couple of other women followed to join her and by the end of the interval the stage was as tidy as it'd been before the fight had begun.

Most folk had rushed out to the foyer, as it had been announced that free beer was being handed out. Athol and Kezia along with Miss Maidstone stayed put. They were wedged in and couldn't have moved even if they had wanted to. The hall was as hot as Hades and folk were sweating buckets, but there wasn't one person except Miss Maidstone who wasn't enjoying the night out and there were so many calling out to each other and so much cheerful laughter that the interval music being played was totally lost. Miss Maidstone kept hitting her fists on her knees. She tried to call out to the women who were tidying the stage to stop but couldn't make herself heard above the noise. Her face had gone scarlet.

After about ten minutes everyone who'd gone out for free beer came pushing their way back in and there were a few arguments over seats, but then the lights in the hall and on-stage went out and for a minute there was a long silence except for some people coughing and the sound of someone at the back being violently sick.

And from the stage there suddenly came a crashing noise and a scream and a lot of loud urgent whispering and the stage lights came back on. The actress who was playing the role of Amanda was lying full stretch across one of the small tables and some man no one had seen before was rushing around pushing lamps over and throwing cushions about and upending the furniture, trying to make the set look as it had done before the interval. Both of them were white-faced and seemed harassed. The actress got to her feet and was rubbing her knees and glaring out at the audience. Most of the audience thought that this was part of the play and started laughing and stamping their feet and clapping.

Once the play got going again the actors kept forgetting their lines. There were long silences. Half the audience didn't seem to have understood what had gone on and the other half thought they saw the joke of the tidied stage and kept laughing so loudly that no one could hear much of what was happening. So the play blundered along to its closing scene with lots of disruption from the audience and eventually the curtains drew together and everyone stood to their feet and applauded like crazy and stomped on the floor and there were shouts of 'Bravo, you jokers!' And before Athol knew it people were pushing and shoving past him and Kezia as if the hall was on fire. Miss Maidstone was sitting leaning forward with her hands over her face, groaning. And as they got up to leave the hall once the crush had eased, Kezia had her brand-new hat knocked off her head and trampled underfoot, and when she got it back she found the false bunch of fruit that had been on top of it had been stolen.

Kezia invited Miss Maidstone back for a cup of tea. She hadn't wanted to go on to the Milk Bar for a flounder and chips supper. Miss Maidstone was in a terrible state. She kept saying over and over that she'd been so looking forward to the play and it had been utterly spoilt for her. She reckoned the whole of Sandspit Crossing should be ashamed of itself, the town was full of Philistines. She'd never been so mortified in all her born days. Eventually Kezia calmed her down with a few aspirins and a lot of arm-patting and kind words and reckoned she'd enjoyed the big night out anyway as everyone had, it'd been a nice change. No one could expect too much from folk in Sandspit, they were just simple sorts and hadn't the education that Miss Maidstone had been able to have. She gave Miss Maidstone several hugs and got Athol to walk her home after a couple of hours.

Norrie had been asleep in his armchair the whole time and hadn't woken up once. He was dead drunk. After Athol returned from seeing Miss Maidstone home, Kezia got him to help haul Norrie off to the bedroom and into his pyjamas. Then just as she was about to put him into bed she stood stock-still for a minute and suddenly started pulling Norrie towards the bathroom. She pushed him through the door across the torn lino and somehow managed to shove him down into the bath, ran back out into the kitchen to fetch a pail of freezing cold water from the tap there and, rushing back through the house, tipped the water all over him before beginning to laugh so much she collapsed on to the toilet seat and just sat there holding her sides.

The following day Norrie had the worst hangover he reckoned he'd ever had to endure. He was sneezing all over his bowl of porridge, claiming that he'd caught influenza and that he was planning to take the day off. Kezia made up his sandwiches as usual and put them, wrapped in grease-proof paper, into his tin and then made him get dressed into his work overalls and he was out the door only an hour later than he normally left. Kezia told him she had all their washing to do as well as the shopping, and Mrs Moina Rout a few doors along had asked to have her sheets washed and dried as she was at her wit's end with bad arthritis in both her knees and her husband up-country visiting a sick relative suffering from piles.

At lunch-time, Norrie came home with the whitest face Kezia and Athol had ever seen on him. He stood in the doorway staring at them sitting at the table enjoying oxtail soup and fried bread and after a minute he said in a real quiet voice that he had some bad news. The supervisor at the furniture factory had announced that the owners were about to close the place down. They'd been working at a loss for the past six months and had endured enough. Norrie, along with all the other blokes who worked there, had been given the sack.

A Picnic at the Bandstand

The same week that Athol Buck turned seventeen, and had been living with Miss Maidstone for two years because Kezia and Norrie were still down south in Wellington seeking out a more productive life, Mrs Kathleen McCauley had a nervous breakdown and went berserk with a bagful of broken bricks. Completely naked, she rampaged down Hinemoa Parade late one night hurling bricks and screaming at the top of her voice that her husband Dan, who'd drowned himself in the sea, had come back to haunt her and was trying to take out his vengeance on her soul. Before she was caught and held down inside a canvas horse-blanket by some burly blokes from the hotel who'd been drinking in there after hours, she'd smashed windows in four houses, as well as the Four Square grocery and the Post Office, and Charlie Gregg (who Miss Maidstone claimed was a Commie spy) was knocked off his bicycle after a brick landed on his head, giving him a black eye and the worst headache he later reckoned he'd ever had in his entire life.

In the following days, after Mrs McCauley had eventually been taken away by ambulance to a mental hospital in Dargaville, police discovered dozens of anonymous hate letters in her empty house. The handwritten letters on lined paper accused her of being everything from a ratbag murderess with a mouth on her like a torn pocket to having become the nastiest miseryguts of a gossip-monger ever known in the whole Northland. There were other things she was accused of in more letters, which the police reckoned were out-and-out slander and possibly obscene. It was said that Mrs McCauley believed the letters had been sent by her husband from beyond the grave. She'd mentioned something to that effect in previous weeks to several people but no one had taken much notice. In the end the letters proved to have been sent by Mr Arthur McArthur, husband of Dolly McArthur whom Mrs McCauley had been intimidating and bad-mouthing for years and who had been shoved into the fake marble counter at the butcher's when caught up in Kathleen McCauley's bad-livered cross-fire. Legal action was ear-wagged about until the whole business fizzled to nothing. Folk in Sandspit had too many other worries of their own. Times were tough.

Athol had moved into Miss Maidstone's house shortly after Norrie Buck had lost his job at the small furniture factory that overlooked Comfort Street. The factory was now closed and abandoned and due to be pulled down. Dry rot in its walls was causing it to be a hazard to adventure-seeking children. Norrie and Kezia had made up their minds within days of Norrie's sacking to head off down to Wellington to seek work and a new home. They'd sold all the furniture and locked up the house. Athol was to keep his eye on it. They were to send for Athol as soon as they'd got settled, but times had become even harder for them once they were on the road. Kezia ended up in Hamilton Hospital when her appendix burst and she'd nearly died, and after she'd been released fit and well again Norrie drove into the back of a cattle-truck along the Desert Road and broke his pelvis, so it was months before they even reached Wellington. Since then it had been one dead-loss disaster after another, according to Kezia's fortnightly letters to Athol. After two years she was still writing to him every so often, claiming that she and Norrie were not yet in any position to support him. So he carried on living at Miss Maidstone's house, in her spare room, working days at the Library and helping Mr Ritter some evenings in his backyard by planing squares of totara wood, on which the dead stuffed possum arrangements were mounted before being trucked off to Wellington to be sold. Athol never ventured inside Mr Ritter's house. He refused to talk back to him about his plans for the Chapel of Enduring Masculinity which were still on Mr Ritter's private agenda. Every moment of his spare time when he wasn't working, Athol spent with Miss Maidstone. They'd become the closest of friends.

On Wednesday evenings at seven o'clock Miss Maidstone would pin her straw hat to her thin, greying hair and pull on a lace shawl over her best frock, which she claimed to have bought off an exiled Russian princess in Auckland. With one arm through Athol's and her huge hand-knitted shopping-bag hanging over the other, she and Athol stepped out along Comfort Street and around the corner to the Majestic Picture Theatre. They'd been going to the seven-thirty show every Wednesday evening for a year, and seen a great many shows good and bad. Always sitting in the same two seats five rows from the front, they'd watch the show eating Miss Maidstone's home-made popcorn and sometimes toffee lumps with raisins which she'd also cooked at home, wrapped in strips of grease-proof paper and placed at the bottom of her bag beneath a tartan blanket that Miss Maidstone never failed to place over her knees. There was never any heating in the Majestic. The place was as draughty as a long-abandoned farm dunny. But the whole theatre had been fumigated six months ago and fleas in the horsehair seats were mostly gone.

Going to the picture show once a week and sometimes again on Saturday night, if there'd been a change in the programme and they could afford the extra cost, was the highlight of the week. It also helped to keep Miss Maidstone's worries about her sister Ursula in check. Ursula Maidstone, retired from having been a Catholic missionary's assistant in New Guinea, had been sending letters from where she lived explaining that she was in the throes of painting her ceiling and the walls of her outhouse, to re-create the ceiling of the Sistine chapel in the Vatican. Once she had completed the calling she'd had to undertake the work, she planned to open her house to the public and charge admission. She was working on other ideas too. She was never going to rely on Government handouts again, nor on the meagre pittance the Catholic Church sent her once a month through her having been forcibly retired. According to her letters, she was joining a new age and expecting to get rich.

'Her elevator's stopped going up to the top storey this time,' Miss Maidstone explained to Athol when the first newsletter arrived in the post from Dargaville. 'I'll have to bike down there and sort her out or she'll be in the poo again. She's hardly ever out of it. Mad as Carroll's hatter, lives on bread and scrape and been headed down the toity ever since New Guinea.' Miss Maidstone told Athol that her sister had been kicked out of a mission station in Papua because of some scandal she'd been involved in just before the outbreak of the last war. Athol was never told what the scandal was. Miss Maidstone would not discuss the details with him, as he was far too young. It'd been of a sexual nature and extremely abnormal. Miss Maidstone thought her sister had been going quietly mad for years, feared that one day she would hear of Ursula having done – as she put it – a Mrs McCauley, and also ending up being away with the fairies for the rest of her natural days.

Magdalen and Ursula Maidstone had been brought up by a diabetic aunt, after their parents had been killed in an avalanche while panning for gold in a South Island river. Ursula was five years older than Miss Maidstone. She had been prone to battiness and irresponsible behaviour most of her life. After the aunt had passed away suddenly, Ursula had run off to Australia and somehow had been converted to Catholicism and transported by an amorous priest to the wilds of New Guinea, without Miss Maidstone's having been on hand to intervene. Ursula had in fact disappeared for a year. Miss Maidstone had feared that her sister had been sold into white slavery, until the priest wrote to her on Ursula's behalf. Miss Maidstone and Ursula had never got along. When Ursula eventually returned to New Zealand Miss Maidstone used some of her own money, and the little Ursula had been given, to set her up in a small bach in the sticks outside Dargaville, where Ursula had decided she would settle down to write her memoirs and continue her missionary work on a free-lance, part-time basis with the local Maoris. Nothing came of the latter just as little developed of the former. Yet

Ursula got by and had become almost self-sufficient during the long years of the war, growing food on her land and joining a women's movement that helped out men overseas by sending off supplies and hand-knitted Balaclavas. Miss Maidstone visited Ursula only out of a sense of duty. Ursula was Miss Maidstone's one surviving relative and that was the sole reason for her having anything to do with such a wasted, up-the-chute life, so Athol was told.

The Bucks' house on Comfort Street was up for sale. It had been up for sale for almost a year. The wooden sign nailed to the front gate had become so weather-beaten it could hardly be read. With help from Miss Maidstone, Athol had boarded up all the windows with planks they'd filched overnight from the crumbling furniture factory. Local louts had been using the house as a kind of play fort and it was also rumoured that teenagers were staking out its empty rooms to experiment in sex, though Athol had never discovered any sign of that. He had heard the rumour from Mrs Gipson who ran the Post Office. Every time he'd gone along there to collect the fortnightly letters from Kezia, Mrs Gipson had clacked her teeth about teenage sex orgies being held in his old home as if Athol were personally responsible. Norrie had tried to keep up the house payments for six months, so Kezia had told Athol in early letters. But after a time she never mentioned the house again and one day the sign appeared right out of the blue. But the house remained empty, just as the Bidwell sisters' house on Anzac Avenue also remained empty and left to rot.

Norrie never wrote to Athol himself but sometimes added a few lines to the bottom of Kezia's letters. One week to say he'd found a well-paid job in some factory, only to have Kezia tell Athol in her next letter that the job had merely been an explosion in Norrie's beer-soaked brain. They'd lived in a State house in Wadestown, a private rented house in Khandallah which they'd shared with two Dutch sailors, been a long time in rooms up at Johnsonville, but were now in a small bach they'd found at Scorching Bay and were hoping to take over a milk bar in Seatoun if all went well. Norrie had worked for three weeks as a postman but discovered he had flat feet and had developed horrendous varicose veins from wearing cheap boots. Athol kept losing track of where they were and what they were doing. He was sure a lot of the letters he'd sat down patiently to write every few weeks had not reached them. Kezia never said a word any more about his going down to join them. Somehow Athol had lost interest anyway. Leaving Miss Maidstone, and Sandspit, was something he thought very little about. Sandspit Crossing might be a real backwoods dump and still shaky with threats of the place becoming a haunt for the helpless, but as Miss Maidstone had said about his heading south, there was no sense in sticking his nose into butter if he was going to have to eat dripping for the rest of his life. Kezia and Norrie seemed no better off down in the city. If they'd stayed on in Sandspit and stuck it out they might even have been on to a good trot in time and with some luck Norrie might have started up his own business, despite his inadequacies.

Life in Sandspit had changed for the worse, though not as much as Norrie had predicted. The township was still holding its own. Although a couple of shops had closed down, the Dairy Board factory was still in business. Most of the local shopkeepers were having second thoughts about packing up. The rest of the country didn't seem to be faring much better, if rumours were true. The Government kept announcing that, now the war was history, it was to be a time of plenty for all, so long as there were no slackarses, but there wasn't much reality in that for most, and politicians, as Miss Maidstone pointed out to Athol, always lied through their rotten teeth whatever the weather. Real folk just got on with try-ing to survive as best they could. They'd done so all throughout both wars and the Depression and with talk of rationing being fully lifted there was some hope. The last war had taken its toll and the after-effects were still being suffered. Poor beggars like Dan McCauley who'd fared badly overseas and had come home only to face domestic nightmares might have caught the brunt, but there were sure to be easier days somewhere up front. Folk had only to hold on to their hats and wait for the sunshine. She could never imagine, Miss Maidstone told Athol, living anywhere else. Sand-spit Crossing, for all its faults, and backwoods mentality, offered a certain kind of freedom. Living miles away from the hard core of life, folk were left alone to get on with normal things. With money her aunt had left her which she'd carefully hidden away, and with money that Kezia sometimes sent without letting on to Norrie, she and Athol shouldn't expect too much strife. One day Kezia and Norrie and all those who had abandoned Sandspit might return. Miss Maidstone dreamt of that happening. She loved this part of the country. When her time came to fall off the perch, she hoped that someone would bury her on the hill overlooking the beach, however neglected that part of town now was. There she could rest and look out across the sparkling waters, recalling in spirit all the days of her years in the town where she had been as happy as a lark and had had friends and companionship and books to read.

Miss Maidstone often talked in such a way to Athol on warm evenings when they sat out on her veranda sipping ginger beer she made from her own secret recipe. They would sit quietly, Miss Maidstone in her squeaking old rocking-chair wearing her shawl and Athol sitting on the steps with his back against the veranda struts. They would remain there for hours long after dark had closed in around them, listening to the crickets in the grass and the occasional cries of night-owls. They were special times in Athol's life, and not to be forgotten. Sometimes it was almost as if his mum and dad had never gone away, as if they were just next door sitting out on their own veranda and he'd only have to shout and he would hear Kezia's voice, or he would hear her laughter at some crack Norrie might make. Miss Maidstone wanted them back, and so did he, but he never believed they would return.

Every day Athol sat alone in the Library and he read books about every place and every subject under the sun, and he dreamt away the quiet of those afternoons, with no customers. Miss Maidstone did not work as hard in the Library as she had before Athol became her Assistant. She had taken up wood sculpture, and was creating something in her backyard she kept covered with a tarpaulin and would let no one see. But often she would join Athol at the Library in the early evenings, if he stayed open, and they would take books down from the high shelves and wipe the mildew from them and afterwards while they played gin rummy Athol would tell her of what he'd been reading. Occasionally, during the daytime if it was raining, Granny Barker, who still suffered discomfort from having caught both her breasts in her daughter's wringer, might come by for a good thriller, to keep her mind off pain. Children might even appear. New books turned up from Wellington. On those days Athol could even imagine that his job would last for ever and that it was worthwhile, for it really wasn't much of a job and mostly he had nothing to do. Yet in the two years since he'd been living with Miss Maidstone he'd found a world in books he'd never imagined he would actually enjoy. She'd finally got him away from comics. Reading, Athol discovered, had nothing to do with being a sissy as Norrie had forever sworn was true. Inside himself Athol was waking up to feelings that he didn't fully understand yet, but in a peculiar way he was happy. He never wanted to leave the town just as his best friend Miss Maidstone never wanted to leave. It was familiar and safe and unthreatening and now, after the war, he imagined nowhere else could be better.

When Miss Maidstone announced one morning that she was planning to bike down to Dargaville to check up on her wayward sister, Athol hadn't been too keen on going. Miss Maidstone had suggested he go with her on the back of the Harley-Davidson. It would do them good to get away for a day, she told him. They could close down the Library without anyone noticing and take food for Ursula in the pannier-bags. Miss Maidstone was having to go anyway, she told Athol. She felt an urge to make some attempt to sort Ursula out, before things got out of control. She hadn't been down to see her sister for months. There was a need, though anything Miss Maidstone might have to say about Ursula's hare-brained schemes would be as significant as a pimple on a pumpkin. With Athol's support she might do a better job. So Athol agreed to go with her.

They set out a few days later weighed down by bottles of pre-serves, sausage-meat sandwiches, biscuits, jam jars filled with ginger beer and a special coconut cake, for which Miss Maidstone had been saving the ingredients.

Miss Maidstone never used a crash-helmet while biking on the Harley but she lent Athol a spare pair of aviator goggles she'd bought off Norrie, back when he'd been involved in building the Tiger Moth and had traded them with a travelling salesman for lumber. She tied up her hair in an old woollen scarf and reckoned

Athol should do the same, but he refused. It was a direct route down along the coast road and they plain-sailed the miles until they were passing through Babylon, when they had a rear tyre blow-out and ended up sitting in a ditch. Fortunately they hadn't been travelling flat-out at the time. They'd had to slow down for a herd of Jersey cows crossing a junction. Miss Maidstone got stuck in straight away and fixed the inner tube from a kit she carried across her back in her shopping-bag. The bike wasn't even scratched. They reached the outskirts of Dargaville by mid-morning.

Ursula Maidstone's bach stood on its own along a dirt-track a few miles out of town and was surrounded by bush gone wild with a small stream running past the backyard, from which Ursula fetched her water. She was chopping firewood out front when they reached the bach. Athol thought when he first spotted her that she was a man the way she was holding and using the axe, and when she straightened up she stared at them with one hand shielding her eyes saying nothing at all for a moment, not even smiling. Her lips were turned down at the edges, her hair cropped so short she appeared to be bald. 'Well, kick me in the guts with both feet, if it isn't Madam Muck!' she called out, staring at Miss Maidstone.

Miss Maidstone didn't say a word. She got down off the bike after Athol and started pulling things out from the pannier-bags, not looking up. Ursula stared Athol up and down and he grinned at her but she just started scratching herself and sucking loudly on her teeth.

The bach was a one-room rickety shack with an outhouse and a covered shelter fixed to the side. Inside the shelter stood a tin bath. It was the strangest place Athol had ever seen anyone living in. From the outside it looked adequate enough but very rough, painted in different colours, and there was a large wooden cross tied to the chimney. Indoors there were crucifixes hanging on every few inches of wall. The ceiling was painted blue with what were meant to be angels, or so Athol guessed, but the angels had no eyes. Each had bright-green hair and huge hands with fingers that stretched out and came down the walls to the floor. Their mouths were wide open as if they were screaming. Ursula told Athol that she hadn't been able to lay her hands on the right colours so she'd made do with what she already had. She acted very proud of her handiwork and friendly towards him. She slapped him on the back and winked at him after Miss Maidstone explained who he was. Ursula's face was lined and dark with tan and she looked ancient but her eyes were bright and sharp. The clothes she wore were crumpled and stained and must have once belonged to a very tall man.

Miss Maidstone had developed a deep frown on her bright-red face. She said very little for a long time after asking Ursula how she was. She glanced at Ursula with a strange expression as if she was about to cry.

A few moth-eaten chooks were wandering in and out the open doorway. One of them sat on a nest of dried grass in one corner. There were boxes of seed potatoes and turnips stacked up on the floor in another corner of the room and in the opposite corner stood a four-poster bed covered with grey blankets, on which squatted a mangy-looking dog that snarled when Athol tried to go near. It kept scratching itself. In the centre of the room was a long table that had newspaper all over it. On the newspaper were bunches of carrots and a few cabbages. The carrots were clogged with black earth. The floor was splashed with paint. There were no curtains at the windows.

After they'd stood about staring at each other for a few minutes Ursula told her sister with a queer grin that once she'd finished painting her chapel, as well as the walls of the outside dunny, she was planning to write a letter to the Pope in Rome. She was going to invite him out to New Zealand. He could afford to come as he had roomfuls of money at the Vatican. He could bless the rest of the country after he'd blessed her work, over which she'd had a vision one night when Gabriel had come down from heaven and told her what she must do after having sexual intercourse with her on the four-poster. Her home was to become a shrine so that all the lost and the damned and fallen women like herself could come and find solace. The Pope owed it to her, after the way she'd been treated in Papua. It hadn't been her fault about the mass suicides.

Miss Maidstone just stared and kept nodding her head, but Athol could see that she'd been getting herself all worked up from the moment they'd stepped inside the door. To Athol, what Ursula told her sister sounded even more mental than Mr Ritter's plans for his church in Sandspit. The two of them might even get along well if they got together.

Once Ursula had stopped talking, the sisters started snapping at each other. Ursula kept rushing about finding letters that Miss Maidstone had sent her, dozens of them, and after shaking them in the air she began to rip them up into tiny pieces, and as they dropped to the floor she stamped on them and ground her heels into them with so much noise the chook sitting on its nest suddenly had a fit and went rushing across the floor squawking, disappearing through the door. Miss Maidstone had unpacked all the food she'd brought and was stacking it all on the table. Her hands were shaking. Then before Athol realized what was happening, Miss Maidstone and Ursula were having a shouting-match. They'd sat down at the table and ignored Athol completely, began thumping their fists and bursting into tears, and when Ursula started yelling over and over again about how many lolly nights had been going on between Miss Maidstone and her teenage sugar-baby, Miss Maidstone really lost control. Jumping to her feet and shouting that she should never have come, she accused Ursula of being the most foul-mouthed fiend she'd ever known, and Ursula sat there agreeing, slapping her thighs and laughing in a high-pitched voice. Scared stiff that they were about to come to blows, Athol got up from the orange-box he was sitting on and took off out front as fast as he could. The sisters carried on screeching at each other for a full five minutes before they both fell silent.

As Athol stood in the yard not knowing what to do the dog came creeping out through the open door with its tail between its legs and ran off down the dirt-track. Then Miss Maidstone came charging out, her hair all over her face, shaking with anger and hitting at her sides with her fists. Just as she did so one of the jars of preserves came hurtling through the air and smashed against one of the fence posts. Miss Maidstone said nothing to Athol, wouldn't even look at him. In a moment she had kick-started the bike and he'd clambered up on the back and they were roaring off down the track to the main road. Athol turned his head to look back as they left. Ursula was standing in the doorway with one hand on her hip, laughing. Miss Maidstone didn't stop or even slow down until they were just outside Sandspit and once they'd reached Comfort Street she left the bike lying on its side on the grass verge outside the house after they got off, and ran inside, slamming the bedroom door behind her.

Athol didn't hear a sound from her or even glimpse her again until the next day when he came back from the Library. And then she said nothing at all. She acted as if the visit to her sister hadn't happened. For the next two days she sat at her kitchen table for hours, writing letter after letter and ripping each one up and muttering to herself under her breath, sometimes holding her clenched fists to her face and weeping. All Athol could think of doing was to keep out of her way, as she refused to speak to him. He'd never seen anyone so angry before.

Early one morning a few days later Miss Maidstone knocked on his door and came in carrying a tray of breakfast. On the tray was a bowl of porridge, freshly squeazed orange juice in a jam jar and doorstop toast with dollops of her home-made marmalade. She sat down on the end of the bed and told him how sorry she was that he'd seen such goings on. She was terrified that he would leave her because of what had happened. She believed her sister was finally losing all her faculties but she still loved her deeply, and cared for her. 'I've always been fair game to Ursula,' Miss Maidstone explained. 'She's never needed my help. Never needed anything to do with me. She thinks I'm her rival. It's jungle hour, every time I go there.'

She started to cry and shake and held her hands up to her face, but Athol leant over and pulled them away and held them while she carried on weeping. Eventually Miss Maidstone wiped her eyes after pulling away and told him that her sister was all the family she had. She'd tried hard to make things work, been kind to Ursula and sent her food and had sent her money for years, but all Ursula ever did was to cause her strife and make a mockery of her. She talked for half an hour and wept some more while Athol sat and listened.

After that morning Miss Maidstone did not mention her sister again. She wrote and sent letters to her every day, to which there were never any replies.

Summer had been holding Northland in its dusty grip all through that time. Christmas had come and gone. There was talk of drought and there were fire restrictions and water shortages and the days passed by as slowly as a snails' hundred-yard race. Kezia wrote to Athol that Wellington was a dead loss. Didn't it rot Athol's socks that she'd ended up in the windy capital, the last place on earth she wanted to settle down in. Norrie was drinking even more than he used to, his liver must be shot. He was on the hard stuff now, though he had a steady job and she was putting the pressure on so that Athol might travel down to join them despite their still being broke most weeks. Her letters were filled with complaints and grievance and what she could do if she found a pot of gold. The house they were renting in Titahi Bay was a dead loss and as useless as a Taranaki gate after a tornado. Norrie was out on the ran-tan every night and how was Athol, did he miss his mum who loved him more than anyone else did? Was he in charge of the Library yet?

Athol didn't know what to say in reply. He wrote about the books he was reading and about a Government course he could attend to become a fully fledged librarian that Miss Maidstone had discovered. He said nothing at all about leaving to join them in Wellington. He mentioned his seventeenth birthday, which they'd forgotten. In return Kezia sent a cheap card covered with kisses and damp patches with its price-tag still attached to the back. There was a pound note folded up inside that someone had written 'Rhubarb' on in bright-red ink.

When news came through that Mrs Kathleen McCauley had died of a stroke in the Dargaville mental hospital, a few women turned up at the Library one day when Miss Maidstone was there with Athol, to ask her if she would be interested in helping to organize a summer picnic, to cheer everyone up and to soften the guilt, as no one had been to see the poor sick woman. There were those in town who felt that a good do and a sausage sizzle might make a nice change anyway, bring in a few out-of-towners to help boost trade and morale. Life had been nothing but bad tidings.

Miss Maidstone leapt at the idea. Within days she had taken it all on to her shoulders as if she was in sole charge, which at first upset quite a few of the married women who secretly pitied her because she didn't have a husband. Miss Maidstone rushed about town like a blue-arsed fly organizing this and trying to organize that and before too long that same week had arranged for a Picnic Extravaganza to be held on the grass around the defunct bandstand that had been burnt to the ground in the twenties and stood, rebuilt, opposite Young's Milk Bar and Grill. There was to be a bonfire, and a free sausage for everyone provided by Mr Ritter, who was only too happy to oblige. He was still keen on Miss Maidstone becoming his bride despite the fact that she'd plainly put the mockers on his earlier proposal. Every time they met, Miss Maidstone told Athol, Mr Ritter would leer at her with lust and go cross-eyed.

Miss Maidstone produced notices about the picnic she printed up on the Library Gestetner, organized children to distribute them to all the outlying farms, tacked even more notices up along the Parade without help from anyone and put dozens into folk's letterboxes. She arranged for free balloons and free party hats to be sent from the big McKenzies in Whangarei, writing to them and inviting all their staff to attend the picnic free of charge. There was to be a lolly scramble, community singing, an amateur *Try Your Luck* quiz show with prizes provided by local shopkeepers, a footy match between two teams of the heaviest blokes from the hotel, and a week later she'd even been sent two boxes of fireworks from one of the many friends she claimed to have met on her travels, who owned a factory in Otorohanga.

Even Mrs Boona Gush along Comfort Street, who had lost her husband and daughter and was a hermit, was dragged into the preparations. She was dragged out of her house and dragged about town on Miss Maidstone's arm while everything was fixed up for a lucky-dip stall which Mrs Gush, despite her objections, was going to run after she'd overseen the cooking. Athol hardly saw Miss Maidstone for days while she was rushing here and rushing there, making lists and listing names and cheerfully bullying anyone who happened to be passing her at the time into becoming a part of the whole show. Athol worried himself silly that she was doing all the work just to get her mind off the troubles she'd had with her sister. But he kept his mouth shut. He didn't think she would have heard him anyway even if he did speak up. She was as busy as a one-armed paper-hanger and all over town her voice wafted like an autumn leaf in a breeze.

The day of the Picnic Extravaganza was as sunny and as hot and as dry as all the others that had preceded it. Miss Maidstone was up at five o'clock that morning and off out of the house singing at the top of her voice before Athol had even pulled himself out of bed. She had been writing and posting letters for days in between her hurrying about town, had cleaned all the windows of the house and washed the curtains, and the morning before, just after daybreak, Athol had woken up and looked out of the window and there was Miss Maidstone cutting the front lawn grass with her rusty old push-mower, still dressed in her nightie with her hair flying all over the place and wearing gumboots, singing 'Anchored to the Rock' so loudly that Granny Barker came out on to her porch and yelled at her to shut up. Athol had never even seen his mum and dad rush about so much, and they were years younger than Miss Maidstone. He'd once asked her how old she actually was, but she just laughed and told him a lady never revealed such things, she was as old as her teeth.

By midday there were carloads of folk turning up from out of town, tractors pulling trailers filled with children all dressed up in their best and half the cowsheds in the district must have been deserted. Everyone was heading down the Parade to the bandstand, which had been decorated with hand-made flags and balloons and a huge hand-painted sign which read WELCOME TO THE PARTY. When Athol arrived, Miss Maidstone was on top of a bonfire stack piling up old car tyres that a couple of Norrie's drinking mates from the hotel were throwing up to her. They were shaking their heads and laughing, for Miss Maidstone, while arranging the tyres, was calling out to this person and that person and even cracking the odd joke. She appeared to be in charge of the whole works. A few women stood about watching her as if they thought she'd gone mental, but everyone was acting happy enough. Trestle-tables had been put up under the trees that bordered the grassed-over area and women were rushing back and forth from the Milk Bar with huge plates of scones and potato salad and biscuits. There were bowls of jelly and home-made fudge and fruit salad. Mr Ritter showed up pushing a large pram he'd borrowed off the Barkers, who had fourteen children and owned five prams, most of which had been stacked up on to the bonfire as the wheels were broken. Inside Mr Ritter's pram, each one wrapped in newspaper and attached to a stick, were dozens and dozens of home-made beef sausages. Mr Ritter had slicked back his hair with bay rum and was wearing his best undertaking suit beneath a white pinafore that Mrs Boona Gush had provided and confessed to Athol on the quiet in a quavery voice that he was all geared up and rearing to propose to Miss Maidstone for a second time. He'd even written a little speech he'd worked on all night. He had high hopes that this time he'd hit the jackpot. What he had to say to her would steam her socks off. She was the tallest poppy in the paddock and he wasn't prepared to stand around like a stale bottle of milk any longer, he wanted that woman to be his wife, or his mistress. But as it turned out, Mr Ritter never got a chance even to get close enough to her to say anything at all.

For Miss Maidstone, the Sandspit Picnic Extravaganza was a sheer triumph and one of the proudest days of her life, so she told Athol when it was all over. No one had stopped her from being in charge. She took over the children's games, started up the community singing by handing out song-sheets she'd printed on the Gestetner, refereed the footy match as if she'd been born to it, and made sure that all the food was handed out fairly so that no one was neglected. There were many who made a big fuss over thanking her. Raewyn Scudder's mum had made a posy of violets which Raewyn pinned to the front of Miss Maidstone's purple dress. Athol kept spotting her from a distance with a constant grin on her face. It was hours later in the day when he first saw the lone figure who appeared walking towards him down the middle of Hinemoa Parade. The figure was wearing a man's brown suit, a woolly hat pulled low over the eyes and hiker's boots and was carrying a knapsack across the shoulders. Athol had thought there was something familiar about the figure but it was a while before he realized who it was.

Ursula Maidstone didn't see Athol at all as she passed him and once she'd walked across to the picnic site she remained on the edge of the crowd staring across at her sister with a strange but gentle grin on her face. Miss Maidstone was in the middle of the lolly scramble, making sure that Mr Ritter, who towered over the children so much he looked like the original friendly giant, wasn't making it too difficult for the screeching tykes. Mrs Gipson had made the jacket he wore out of three potato sacks. The jacket was covered in lollies and sixpences tied up in paper. Mr Ritter was running round and round the bandstand chased by dozens of children trying to pull the lollies and sixpences off his jacket, and Miss Maidstone was yelling with laughter as he pounded the turf because his face was as red as a boiled lobster from all the effort and he looked short of a few shillings from the expressions he was pulling. At one point he fell down and was immediately buried by so many children falling on to him that he completely disappeared.

But then for some reason Miss Maidstone happened to look up, straight into the eyes of her watching sister and became very still. She stopped laughing and seemed frozen to the spot, her mouth dropping open enough to catch a dozen flies. Afterwards she told Athol she would never forget that second when she clapped eyes on Ursula across the heads of the pushing, screaming, grabbing children. It was like the brightest ray of sunshine zooming down at her from the sky. Before too many minutes had passed, the two sisters were in each other's arms, crying and hugging and both shouting then laughing at once above the racket. Athol watched them linking arms and hurrying off to a quiet spot, where they sat down under a tree and carried on crying and hugging and talking in whispers. Folk stared and pointed and Mr Ritter stared for a while but no one went over to them. They were left alone for the reunion, as most folk in town knew all about Magdalen and Ursula Maidstone and their rocky relationship. Miss Maidstone had told everyone often enough.

Hours later, once the day's light had faded away and the bonfire was lit and folk had finished dancing, after the fireworks had been let off by Charlie Gregg and Raewyn Scudder's Uncle Frodo, everyone joined hands in a huge circle and sang 'For She's a Jolly Good Fellow' and gave Miss Maidstone cheer after cheer for having been such a good sport. Mr Ritter made a speech, but it wasn't to ask Miss Maidstone to marry him. He said that she was the most tireless, unselfish woman in the whole Northland. Miss Maidstone and her sister were still arm in arm, standing apart from everyone else near the trees. For one brief moment Miss Maidstone turned and stared across to where Athol was sitting on the bandstand steps. Her face was shining brightly, her eyes as jubilant and as elated as if she was walking on the moon.

Invitation to a Vigil

At about the same time Miss Maidstone announced to Athol that she had finished working on the finest modern sculpture she'd been inspired to create in her backyard, and was thinking about planning a grand birthday unveiling to invited guests, Mr Ritter was discovered with his trousers round his ankles committing sodomy with a rapturous Mrs Gipson on top of the Post Office counter.

It was Mrs Ida Grey who discovered the pair. According to what she later told everyone who would listen, she'd been passing the Post Office on her way to attend to her weekly weeding over at the cemetery when she heard a noise that she mistakenly thought was like the sounds she herself had made when Cyril, her old man, had knocked her about. Finding the door unlocked, though it was late in the afternoon and long past closing time, she had barged inside without thinking and in the ensuing chaos had shrieked for so long and so loudly at what she saw she managed to damage one of her own ear-drums, while belting Mr Ritter's bare behind violently with the handle of her late husband's hoe.

The news clashed with Miss Maidstone's verbal invitation for half the town to attend Athol's nineteenth birthday celebration at her home so she could also unveil her sculpture called 'Hope Springs Eternal'. The shock and astonishment of what Ida Grey had accidentally exposed and hadn't stopped flapping her gums about openly to all and sundry for a week was so great it ruined any chances of Miss Maidstone's carrying out her plans. No one showed the slightest interest.

The sculpture, as Miss Maidstone had painstakingly explained to Athol, was modern art, dedicated to the famous New Zealand sculptress Raeleen Cressell who'd lived in Sandspit Crossing. The piece, which she believed was her most daring to date and made entirely from Sandspit beach driftwood, was a call for renewed determination that Sandspit fight the escalating threat of being doomed to extinction from apathy, as well as being a personal statement that Raeleen Cressell's disappearance back in the early thirties would one day be solved. In the last couple of years Miss Maidstone had begun also to believe that many folk were losing all interest in Sandspit Crossing as a township. Quite a number of families had already decided to move away completely as soon as they could, down to the city for an easier life in the new decade, where jobs were being handed out like lollies at a party.

The advent of the sculpture, which Miss Maidstone had been hoping might be transplanted to a spot near the bandstand in honour of her standing in town, was passed over and quickly forgotten by wagging tongues for the revelation that Mrs Gipson, a widow and highly respected though a gossip, had been indulging in what many reckoned was sheer perverted sex, with a man who should have known better and who nobody had ever imagined was festering with abnormal longings. After all, he'd once been an undertaker and was now the town's esteemed butcher. Many had set store on Mr Ritter as an example of simple New Zealand respectability.

Over the next few weeks the talk about Mr Ritter never stopped. He was blamed and put on the outer by many folk. Yet he carried on opening up the shop every day, and as there was no other place anyone could buy their meat, he didn't really have any worries about losing trade. Every time he walked down Hinemoa Parade though, blokes would nudge each other and wink and some might snigger out loud a bit, while women crossed to the other side of the street with angry faces and averted eyes. Sodomy wasn't something that went on every day and had been unheard of in New Zealand up until then. A few women hadn't at first understood what Mrs Ida Grey had been so anxious to communicate by talking about it in such detail, yet everyone realized it was something filthy and not normal. As she'd even told Miss Maidstone one morning, having worn out almost all other ears, sexual matters between normal married couples were difficult enough, without blokes finding other ways to enjoy their Vita Brits. Mr Ritter and Mrs Gipson might both be widowed and free-choosing adults as she was herself, but there was a limit to degradation. Sodomy was going far beyond any boundary. They hadn't even locked the door.

Athol was told by Miss Maidstone the same night that Mrs Grey should look into her own backyard before she nosed into other folk's passions. Mr Ritter had had a need. If Mrs Gipson was happy and willing enough to provide relief, then so be it. Complaining about it wouldn't cook the sausages. Mrs Ida Grey had always been far too interested in the seamier side of life. Some folk said she'd actively enjoyed the way her own husband had used her as a human football when he'd been alive and drunk, it'd possibly given meat to her vegies. And Miss Maidstone was eternally grateful to Mr Ritter that he had at long last turned his sights away from her. She'd always suspected that he possessed dark desires.

Mrs Gipson left town some time after that and no one stopped her or asked her to stay. The running of the Post Office was passed over to Jack Lamb, who ran Young's Milk Bar and Grill with his wife Beryl. She had been creating a lot of talk herself, as she was heading down the gin track. Jack Lamb had always kept his eye on the Post Office as it was a business he'd been hankering after for years, so the place was closed for only a week during the awkward transition. Mr Ritter stayed put with pursed lips. He had nothing to say to anyone.

Eventually the scandal died its death and was mostly forgotten. There was new talk that the Dairy Board was to close its factory. Then there was more talk that the rumour was just a piece of panic-mongering, but the mud stuck and it was all everyone across town was flapping about. For if the factory closed, the future to Sandspit was as dim as a five-watt bulb would be to a packed-out Masonic Hall. As Miss Maidstone told Athol, without the work, the backbone of the town, the hard-working blokes of the Dairy Board factory, might just as well suck off into the sunset.

Miss Maidstone had taken up wood sculpting in a serious way at the same time as her success with the Picnic Extravaganza two years before. She told Athol she'd had long-term longings to be a sculptress like Raeleen Cressell. Most of what she'd created was now destroyed, burnt up in backyard fires, as nothing until she'd hatched up 'Hope Springs Eternal' had seemed to satisfy her need for artistic perfection. She had thrown herself into the sculpting with tools she'd inherited from Norrie Buck and with as much passion as she wrote letters or had run the Library, which she now left entirely to Athol. Since Ursula had suddenly shipped herself off to Australia a year ago after coming to the conclusion that New Zealand gave her nothing but stiff rotten luck and a twisted outlook, Miss Maidstone had, as she put it to Athol, been consumed with a red-hot need to create something beautiful with her hands. She spent hours tramping along the coast searching for driftwood and dead trees, was often seen by folk marching along down the Parade to the beach in her gumboots at dawn with her bow-saw balanced across her shoulders and wearing a dreamy look on her face. To most folk in town she had now officially retired, though she was thought too young to apply for a pension. Her triumph over the Picnic Extravaganza had lasted for a fair time after the event was history. During that time her reputation had changed from her being the brainy but dippy spinster who loved books more than people to someone folk might expect a lot from, an organizer, a tough shining cuckoo who could get things done when things needed to be done. It had given even a few folk who didn't care a stuff about community spirit a lot of respect for her. Yet it hadn't made her any new friends, or more popular, and memory had faded, so most of the time when Athol wasn't at the Library or helping to paint the outside walls of Mrs Boona Gush's house, he was the only company Miss Maidstone had. In all Sandspit they were probably the oddest-looking friends, yet they were rarely apart. And always, each would know where the

other was, at any time of the day. No one thought it peculiar, for
Athol had grown up right next door to Miss Maidstone. Everyone
knew that Kezia Buck, before she and Norrie abandoned town, had
made Miss Maidstone swear on the Bible that she would take care of
their only son, because they were going away to discover and grab a
better life before they sent for him. That was what family was all
about.

Kezia and Norrie had finally settled down in a solidly built house
on a quarter-acre section in Lower Hutt, which was, in the new
decade, a blossoming place and heaven for blokes with brown
fingers. Norrie had landed a tip-top job as a supervisor for a
woodworking factory that built cheap housing, housing that was
transforming the Hutt Valley into an area of the lower North Island
that even some Sandspit folk were talking of moving down to. Kezia
had finally got the message that Athol didn't want to leave Sandspit
Crossing. Though every so often in her letters to him she reckoned
she could not for the life of her understand why. She and Norrie
were up easy street, living off the pigs back down in the Hutt. They
were even thinking about buying a brand-new car as well as a
modern refrigerator with a separate freezer. Kezia sent Athol money
some months. He hadn't been down to see her and Norrie except
for one visit. He passed the money over to Miss Maidstone. Kezia
sent Athol new shirts and trousers and woollen socks, and for his
nineteenth birthday there arrived a second-hand three-piece serge
suit in mustard green which Athol hadn't yet worn as he never went
anywhere that required a suit.

Athol was now officially in charge of the Library. He had passed
an informal written examination after studying for a few weeks. As
far as Sandspit was concerned, he was the new Librarian and
following in Miss Maidstone's footsteps. Folk were even beginning
to use the Library as it was supposed to be used, going to Athol for
advice despite his youth and his way of keeping to himself, which
many thought a little queer. They simply put that down to his
living with Miss Maidstone.

Raewyn Scudder, who years before had allowed Roy Gonda to be
more than just the boy down the street, had finally got herself really
pregnant by Charlie Gregg, twice her age and still suspected of

being a Commie spy. Contrary to what Raewyn wanted, the two of them were married off and Charlie was supposed to have drunkenly announced at the reception, held in the Scudders' backyard, that despite Raewyn's having features as coarse as a goat's behind, she'd probably make him a decent enough wife. He was on the top of the heap at long last. They'd gone off on honeymoon to Cape Reinga for two weeks with Raewyn's mum. When they got back, Mrs Scudder made Charlie move his possessions from his clapped-out old bach near the beach into the Scudder household on Anzac Avenue, so she could keep a close eye on him. Every Friday night when the shops stayed open late, Charlie, Raewyn and Raewyn's mum walked up and down the Parade arm in arm. Charlie, at Raewyn Gregg's side, looked like a new man, shaved and clean with a short back and sides and darned socks. It was a success story, so everyone claimed. It cheered folk up and helped a little to soften the blow, when the announcement was made one morning that the Dairy Board was definitely planning to close down its factory and move it south, but was to postpone the closure for at least twelve months. The news was as welcome as a grunting pig at a funeral. There was a general stirring up of aggravation at first until a town meeting was organized to discuss the matter. Miss Maidstone was approached to see if she would start up a local petition, but she was too busy putting the finishing touches to a Save Our Sandspit appeal, which she'd decided was going to be an important challenge in her life and involve the whole country and not just Sandspit Crossing. The idea for the local petition was passed on to Curly Barker, Granny Barker's second son, who'd fathered fourteen children and had worked at the Dairy Board factory ever since he'd been released from a TB sanatorium in Kawakawa with a clean slate.

Miss Maidstone's idea for her own appeal was to write letters to every Member of Parliament in Wellington, as well as to the Prime Minister, begging for financial help so that Sandspit could be put on the map and become a tourist centre catering for overseas visitors, a good healthy place for all sorts to start up new businesses and forge a worthwhile life. She'd never had any time for politicians but, as she confessed to Athol one night, they were there and every last one of the buggers was paid to sort out problems, and she could also tell lies, grovel, cheat and pull the wool as well as the next bloke if she had to. She'd planned a money-making scheme, which was to involve sending envelopes to every important person in the country, inviting them to send the envelopes back with donations sealed inside which would be kept safe by Jack Lamb at the Post Office until such time as there was enough money to create a Cash Committee. The Cash Committee could then decide how the donations should be spent. Mrs Boona Gush had offered her help to stuff and lick once Miss Maidstone had printed up all the letters. Miss Maidstone had already made an appeal-fund stand out of cardboard. She was hoping to nail it to the front door of the Masonic Hall so that local folk passing by could see that the appeal wasn't a load of humbug.

Save Our Sandspit took off in a big way. Within a few weeks envelopes came in from Wellington and from Auckland and even as far away as Christchurch and, as each donation arrived, the amounts, which were mostly small, were entered into a ledger with the date and who had sent it, the money placed inside a shoe-box and hidden away at the Post Office under Jack Lamb's care. Jack Lamb had once been a private detective years before he married Beryl and was an honest bloke, so it was thought, the perfect choice to be a money guardian. As the weeks went by, the donations grew less and less though there'd been a fair few pounds sent, enough to make a start. On Miss Maidstone's suggestion Jack Lamb was considering the possibility of having a separate safe installed, just for the appeal money, on hire from a friend of Miss Maidstone who ran a business down in Wainuiomata importing safes from England. But, unbeknown to Jack Lamb, or anyone else, someone in town with hoggish intent was keeping a peeled eye on his movements and whereabouts and it certainly wasn't so Jack could be given a pat on the back for being a good keen bloke.

Miss Maidstone's reputation for being someone who could get organized and pull Sandspit Crossing up the gumption ladder had gone out of fashion in some quarters of the townsfolk's memory. The Save Our Sandspit appeal jogged a few tired brains. During the few weeks that she kept the appeal alive and hot on the coals she was greeted and called out to, everywhere she went. She told Athol she felt a bit like a hawk in an onion sack as, going around from house to house spreading the glad tidings, she'd become a bit panicked. Folk were starting to look on her as a kind of saviour. She didn't really need that situation on her mental plate. She wanted to keep Sandspit alive but she didn't have a desire to become the Madam Muck her sister Ursula had often named her in the past, before Ursula had come to her senses. She thought that a lot of Sandspit folk were, as she put it, Handovers – they wanted the town to survive and were scared to buggery that they'd have to move on somewhere else, but she'd been the one shoved into holding the reins of power, letting the unables off the hook. Folk could rely on her to solve all the problems and blame her if it all fell flat. Athol didn't point out that the appeal had been her own idea. Miss Maidstone was relishing all the attention, despite moaning about it in a humble way. It was to be a long time before Athol realized how much Miss Maidstone really loved the town, that without it she might want to throw in the towel. She said nothing to him about how she truly felt, she rode the bull through china with the appeal and it became the most important task she'd ever taken on, so she kept claiming. But while she rushed here and there and wrote letters and made lists and jollied up the ungenerous, just around the corner along the street, disaster sat waiting, flexing its greedy fingers.

After she was named official secretary of the appeal fund, Miss Maidstone got a letter one day from the female followers who organized and held the annual vigil for the disappeared sculptress Raeleen Cressell. The women were organizing yet another gathering at Raeleen Cressell's bach near the beach, and, as Miss Maidstone had now retired from the Sandspit Library, was prominently involved in the attempt to redeem the town's diminishing lifeblood and had begun, according to rumour, to do some sculpting herself, she was invited to attend that year's vigil, as one of the ten followers of the Female Icon had passed away.

When Athol came back from the Library that day, Miss Maidstone was more excited than he had seen her for months, her eyes sticking out like eggs in the wrong nest. She was over the moon and dancing about the news. Along with the letter was an official invitation printed on a white card with a black border, which was worded so strangely it sounded to Athol as though Raeleen Cressell was still alive and would be at the vigil in person despite having been nothing but a memory for years and presumed dead. Miss Maidstone's longing to be asked to attend one of the annual functions had almost dried up. She'd given up hope. So before Athol had even arrived home she'd written out her reply, that she would be turning up at two o'clock on the following Saturday afternoon with a food plate as requested and a genuine sense of artistic honour.

From then on it was all she could talk or think about from dawn until dusk. Any donations to the appeal fund and even some canvassing were shoved on to Mrs Gush, who'd lately come out of her hermit shell through Miss Maidstone's care and attentions. Having been in mourning for ten years for her dead husband and daughter, she'd let their memory be borne off by the wind of personal change, jumping in with both feet to Save Sandspit, and every Friday night Mrs Gush was to be seen standing on the corner of Hinemoa Parade and Comfort Street brandishing a placard which read SANDSPIT SALVATION – ARE YOU DOING YOUR BIT? ALL DONATIONS WELCOME.

Before too many days had passed Miss Maidstone had told half the town that she'd received the invitation and what a great honour it was, despite the fact that no one else was interested in going to a wake for a dead sculptress. As some pointed out, Raeleen Cressell had only been a New Zealander after all and a woman, she couldn't have been that famous, no one would have known who she was overseas in places where real artists lived. But Miss Maidstone marched about the house and about town with the biggest grin on her face that Athol had ever seen her sport, and he did his best not to grow tired of her telling him that she was the proudest woman in the whole country, that she had secretly worshipped the great sculptress deep down where it mattered. If Sandspit chose to ignore past genius in its midst, then it was their bad loss, she said. Raeleen Cressell's mystic poetry had been published to acclaim in England as well as in America and, dead she might be, but her spirit lived on and it lived amongst them, here in this tin-can ignorant town where the woman had breathed and created and nurtured her enduring words and statues of beauty. There was no way that her invitation had been sent only because the women followers wanted to boost flagging interest, so Mrs Enid Mills, who made her old man sleep in the backyard shed, had pointed out to her. Miss Maidstone had been invited, she told Athol, because she was Miss Maidstone, a person of standing in Sandspit Crossing. She was planning to make the most of it while she could, and blow the mangy mongrels who scoffed.

Athol had been down to visit Kezia and Norrie in the last year. He had hitched rides all the way down and returned on a Newman's coach which Norrie had reluctantly paid for. Miss Maidstone had reckoned Athol was a brave soldier, travelling all that way on his own to see the mum and dad who'd abandoned him, albeit temporarily. Wellington had scared him with all its people and noise and drunks all over the streets, and just after he arrived and was looking for the Lower Hutt train platform, a huge woman wearing a veil over a wide-brimmed hat and with a face like an uncooked pikelet had sidled up to him and whispered that she'd charge him only a few pounds to do something sexual with her that he'd never heard of and which she swore would change his whole life. When he later told Kezia about the encounter she just laughed and told him there were good-time women like her all over Wellington, it didn't meant anything. He might've learned something.

Kezia had dyed her hair blonde. She was working as a barmaid at a hotel near where she and Norrie lived. She had changed so much Athol hardly knew who she was. When they took him out for a meal and a few beers that first night she asked him not to call her Mum any longer, as she'd lied about her age to all their mates.

Norrie never stopped drinking the whole time Athol was visiting, though he and Kezia seemed happy enough. They were making a lot of money at the Trots every Saturday night, so Kezia told him. They loved horse-racing. Neither she nor Norrie asked Athol about Sandspit Crossing or Miss Maidstone or even how his job was going.

Long after the visit was over and he was back in Sandspit he decided not to go down again. He felt his mum and dad had grown away from him with their new life. They went out every night with their friends, were planning parties all the time and never got up until after midday, Norrie had time off work and Kezia said she needed all the beauty sleep she could get, life was hectic. Out the back of the house were so many beer crates piled up that Athol joked about Norrie's building a spare room with them one day, which didn't go down very well. Kezia accused him of becoming a snob, that he should get with it and jazz up his ideas or he'd end up as duff as a collapsed paling fence. Athol still loved them both and he missed them, but they were not the mum and dad he remembered from Comfort Street. When he left, neither of them even came to see him off at the bus station. Kezia was having her hair bleached and permed in a new modern way at her best friend's salon across at Normandale and Norrie was off out to help a mate, who'd lost an arm and a leg in the war, to lube up his Morris Minor. Athol reckoned he didn't belong with Kezia and Norrie any longer. They seemed like a couple of happy-go-lucky strangers whom he had once known in a different life.

He carried on writing to Kezia every couple of weeks from his room in Miss Maidstone's house after his return and he walked across to their old house every so often to make sure that no one had broken in. The house was almost derelict now, paint peeling from the weatherboards and the roof gone rusty. No one had bought it. He sat on the veranda and dreamt about days that were long gone. At nineteen he felt that he must be grown up or had to pretend to be and that the past, when Norrie and Kezia had cared for him, was so far behind it'd been another life. He remembered that past as a dream which, sometimes when he sat there, made him cry without his knowing the reason for it. They were all happy enough with the way things were, no one was complaining. He loved Miss Maidstone as he loved still living in Sandspit, and he didn't want the feeling to end as it had ended for Kezia and Norrie. He was growing up fast and was on his own but something inside him wanted to hold on to the days that were ended.

On the day of the vigil at Raeleen Cressell's bach Miss Maidstone dressed herself in a full-length purple frock, real silk stockings, a pill-box hat and veil, white elbow gloves and a fox fur around her shoulders. She told Athol she'd inherited the outfit from the aunt who had taken care of her and Ursula and had left everything in a will. Miss Maidstone had gone on and on to Athol about his going with her for company, as she was much too nervous to turn up alone. In the end he agreed. He put on the suit that Kezia had sent him, along with a white shirt that had belonged to Mrs Boona Gush's husband, and a tie that Miss Maidstone had hand-made from part of an old curtain. They were ready a whole hour before the time they were due at the Female Icon's bach.

Raeleen Cressell had become nationally famous for a series of statues called 'Men without Privates', the first one of which stood fifteen foot tall and had been taken on show around the country by a group of post-suffragette women on the back of a Ford truck. For years the statue had stood on a hill overlooking the sea at Baring Head, near Wellington. It had been made from seven different kinds of native wood. No one knew if it was supposed to represent a Maori man or a Pakeha man but it was meant to portray, whichever it was, the male body with its anger, virility and the main cause of female strife taken away. It had caused a national outcry from important New Zealand males when it had first appeared, and even a certain amount of violence.

The sculptress had started up a women's movement in the early 1920s, which had set out to knock male aggression on the head and to encourage a new, non-political age of Female Confidence. At least, this was how Miss Maidstone explained it all to Athol one night while they were sitting in the dark on her veranda sipping ginger beer and eating a plateful of Melting Moments she'd just baked. The sculptress and mystic poet had had thousands of female followers until the fateful day she'd disappeared and was believed by just as many to have been raped and murdered. A country-wide search had been made for her, but no trace of her whereabouts was ever established. It was eventually bandied about that she'd been attacked and killed by a group of women-hating bachelor farmers down in Taranaki, who lived together and farmed in the nude, and, it was rumoured, were keen on younger men joining them to till the soil, as well as engaging in sexual activities that were unmention-able. But the allegations fizzled out, Raeleen Cressell's body was never found and the bach that she'd lived in was kept exactly the same as it had been when she'd disappeared by her closest admirers, who still waited in hope for her to reappear. According to Miss Maidstone, Raeleen Cressell's poetry, some of which had been written in a language new to mankind, had been published in translation by almost every civilized country across the globe except New Zealand, and after it was officially acknowledged that she must be dead, she was named a New Zealand Icon, from which time her largest and most impressive statue of all the 'Men without Privates' she'd created was reproduced in bronze to replace the original at Baring Head, which had suffered from wind, exposure, woodworm and having teenagers' initials carved on it, and it was now in the Wellington Museum behind glass after months of restoration.

Miss Maidstone had been specially chosen to attend the vigil because one of the Icon's ten followers who, she told Athol, were called Apostles, had died from kidney failure and there was a good chance that Miss Maidstone might replace her. Going to the vigil was to be, she hoped, the proudest day of her life. Even though she'd eventually been told by half the town that it was a dead cert that the women involved in keeping the legend alive were nothing more than a group of long-past-the-post pea-brains, who probably wore iron undies, hated all men and were townies to boot. There were quite a few blokes and women in Sandspit, Miss Maidstone confessed to Athol, who actually remembered Raeleen Cressell, having met her in person and hated her, reckoned she'd either been in league with the Commies just as Charlie Gregg was supposed to be or completely off her rocker. She'd been warned off getting involved. Mr Ritter had even confided in her when she'd gone into the butcher's for some fresh egg stuffing that it might prove to be downright dangerous, though he could talk after what he'd been up to, and she'd put him straight over that.

When Miss Maidstone and Athol arrived at the bach, the woman who met them at the door, who said her name was Mrs Valeria Kingston-Smith and who had a complexion like week-old boiled mutton, made it clear that Athol wasn't welcome and pointed out to Miss Maidstone in a stiff voice that he hadn't been invited. The vigil was for women only. No man had set foot inside the bach for going on twenty years. Miss Maidstone kept saying how sorry she was, over and over again, that she'd been far too

jelly-hearted to come alone and she'd vouch for Athol Buck, he ran
the local Library and wasn't anything like other young lads of his
age, he was gentle and different. After staring him up and down
with a maggoty look Mrs Kingston-Smith said well, fair enough,
Athol could come in as long as he kept quiet and wasn't disruptive.
He could help hand out the tea and do the dishes after, though Miss
Maidstone had put her and the other Apostles in a tight spot.

As Miss Maidstone said to Athol on their way back to Comfort
Street once it was all over, the 'vigil' had been a huge disappointment and possibly an insult to Raeleen Cressell's memory and
well-documented strength. She'd been expecting something myste-
rious or exotic, a day to grab her soul and change it for ever. But the
whole shebang turned out to have been even more dreary than the
Women's Institute afternoons her aunt had dragged her off to when
she'd been a teenager.

The bach was made up of four rooms, each of which was empty,
just bare boards and mildew on the ceilings and signs of an over-
population of mice. In the main room the nine Apostles, who were
all past sixty and had more wrinkles than a herd of goats, were
sitting about on metal foldaway chairs dressed in what looked to
Athol to be converted bedsheets with lace aprons. Their outfits
were, it was explained, replicas of what Raeleen Cressell had worn
when she was sculpting. The women were all knitting or sewing
and talking at once but went stone-cold quiet when Miss Maidstone
swept in with Athol on her arm. One of the women let out a stifled
gasp and covered her mouth with her thimbled fingers, and a
younger woman who was just entering from the kitchen acted so
perturbed she dropped the porcelain teapot she was carrying and it
smashed on the floor, splashing hot tea in all directions. Athol felt
overdressed and foolish. Miss Maidstone's face at first had gone a
strange purple shade. For a while the atmosphere in the room
could've been sliced with a knife. But then Miss Maidstone shook
herself and smiled and went about being introduced, shaking hands
and saying what must have been all the right things and soon even
Athol was attended to. He was sat down in the corner and handed a
cup of tea and a slice of banana cake. Before very long he was being
used by a woman from Dunedin, who told him her name was Mrs
Voda Waterman, to ball up some home-dyed wool by holding the

yarn over his outstretched arms. While she wound the wool she told him all about her son who was an engineer with the Merchant Navy and went out shooting wild pigs with his one-legged father when he was home on leave.

As Miss Maidstone, and Athol indirectly, were told, much of Raeleen Cressell's personal possessions had been sold off to help keep the Apostles, who worshipped the Icon's memory, from having to sell her land. What hadn't been sold was stored in their own homes all over the country where other meetings and fund-raising events were held. They were currently trying to get Raeleen Cressell's mystic poetry republished in America and launched for the first time in New Zealand and in New Guinea. There was a lot going on. The vigil at the now empty bach was simply a gesture, in the hope that one day the awful mystery of her disappearance might be solved. For years it had been thought that the Icon might show up, that she wasn't dead at all, but hope had faded long ago and there was now under discussion a plan to open a museum down south in the great woman's memory. Where that was to be, no one had yet decided.

After a lot of talking and more cups of tea, when Miss Maidstone told the room all about her own life and her troubles with wayward Ursula, Athol helped Mrs Waterman carry in a huge iced cake with birthday candles on it which were duly lit and blown out and was to commemorate Raeleen Cressell's birthday the week before. Then rare photographs of the Icon and even rarer handwritten poems she'd composed were passed around and talked about, but Athol wasn't allowed to touch them. He looked at them over Miss Maidstone's shoulder. A few of the poems were read out loud by Mrs Dorothy Dakota, who'd been born in New Jersey, America, but had come out to live in New Zealand to be near her idol's birthplace. She took a shine to Athol and spent twenty minutes telling him all about the four husbands she'd married and buried but that she'd ended up having more satisfaction from the company of women. Most men, she told him, were a sad disgrace to humanity. Then the minutes of the last vigil were read out by Mrs Kingston-Smith, and once that was finished they all trooped out into the backyard to plant a small ti-tree bush and listen to a reading of one of Raeleen Cressell's most famous poems, 'Sisters Gathering at the

Flaming Phallus'. The poem didn't make any sense at all to Athol.
A lot of the verses were, as Miss Maidstone whispered in his ear,
based on talking in tongues which she didn't explain the meaning
of and it wasn't something Athol knew anything about. Some of
the lines made him blush.

Everyone turned out to be very friendly. To Athol the women
were not much different from those he had met in Wellington with
Kezia. It was like being in a roomful of favourite aunts, and the only
woman there who had been rude, called Miss Marga Binns, had
ended up confessing to Miss Maidstone that she felt she'd known
Miss Maidstone all her life and she was really keen on getting the
recipe for her ginger beer which had been enthusiastically discussed. When Miss Maidstone was introduced to Marga Binns by
Mrs Kingston-Smith, the woman said in a loud whining voice, not
looking at Miss Maidstone for more than a second: 'And have you
also invited anyone interesting to be a replacement for the dear
departed, Mrs KS?' which had caused Miss Maidstone's face to turn
to fire and worked her up quite a lot.

It was probably the most boring afternoon Athol had ever spent,
though he never let on. Like Miss Maidstone, he'd expected the
vigil to be something quite different, and not just a gathering of
gum-flapping old hens. As nice as they were to him, he couldn't
wait to leave, though afterwards Miss Maidstone was full of it, or
acted as if she was, how she had made such bonzer new friends,
however big the disappointment was that such a unique figure in
New Zealand's cultural history should be remembered in such an
ordinary, tea-partyish way. It didn't seem quite right, she kept
saying. She had asked to have her name put forward to be an
Apostle but cracked on that she wasn't sure she could cope with the
annual excitement. Raeleen Cressell had been one of the strongest,
most forthright women in all New Zealand and it was a distortion,
she told Athol, of what the Icon had stood for, and fought for, all
those years ago. Her followers had even sold off most of the less
well-known sculptures. Many of them had been shipped across to
England and North Africa, where her work was revered. New
Zealand never appreciated her own, even after they were dead,
except if they were Rugby players, for no one except for these nine
women probably wanted to remember the creator of 'Men Without

Privates', nor, she added, did the country or the males-only Government care. She began to lose interest in becoming an Apostle after a
few days had gone by. She never heard officially about it, though she
assumed she was part of the team – an honorary Apostle, as she put it
– despite the whole idea being pigs' poop and treacle, she told
Athol, and as boring as the Budget. Yet she didn't stop talking
about the afternoon for days until she was all talked out, and was
back to throwing herself into Save Our Sandspit again, with Mrs
Boona Gush.

Soon little more was mentioned about the vigil at Raeleen
Cressell's empty bach. Miss Maidstone had been presented with a
small photograph of the Icon as they left. She kept it on the mantel
for a while, until one day Athol noticed that it wasn't there any
longer. One afternoon, just before dusk, Athol looked out through
the kitchen window and there was Miss Maidstone holding a can of
kero, splashing it over her wooden statue, 'Hope Springs Eternal'.
After she'd thrown a lit match and the whole statue was throwing
up sparks into the darkening sky, Miss Maidstone stood there with
both hands on her hips, wearing her gumboots and an old Balaclava
pulled over her hair. She began to sing 'Mothers of Salem' in a
quiet voice that slowly grew louder and louder and then faded away
once the statue was no more than a pile of smoking ashes and the
sky had completely stolen away the light of the day.

The following week, late on a Saturday night, Charlie Gregg,
who was said to have been as drunk, earlier that night, as anyone in
town had ever seen him and at his wit's end having had to live with
his new bride's mum as much as with Raewyn, broke into the Post
Office, knocked Jack Lamb over the head with a mallet and tied
him up with rope. Stealing all the Save Our Sandspit donation
money, he fled town in a stolen van, accompanied by Jack Lamb's
gin-worshipping wife Beryl, with whom it was later disclosed Charlie Gregg had been having torrid and secret sex for more than five
years.

The Unspeakable Sausage Saga

Seven days before the Dairy Board finally announced the shutting down of its factory altogether, Mrs Enid Mills's husband Horace completely dismantled his backyard shed, after sitting the whole day on top of it with an air rifle, talking to himself flat-out and shouting obscenities. During that night he moved the shed lock stock and barrel on the back of a borrowed truck to the grass in front of the bandstand, after turning the garden hose on full blast and aiming gallons of water through opened windows into every room of the house where he and Mrs Mills lived, behind Comfort Street.

Mrs Enid Mills had been away visiting her elder sister at the time. Her sister was married to a Samoan farmer down at Mitimiti who'd been accused of sending his unpaid taxes to relatives back home for over ten years. Time and the taxman had finally caught up with him. There was to be a trial at Whangarei. The news had been in all the newspapers for weeks. Mrs Enid Mills had been full of it, told everyone across town she was to be a character witness at the trial and she'd bought a whole new outfit to wear for the occasion.

The following day Horace Mills bought all the wallpaper and

carpet squares he could lay his hands on, plus an old oil-burning refrigerator, and announced that he was setting up house inside the shed, as his wife made him sleep in it every night and he felt more at home there. He had had it, as far as his life with Mrs Houseproud Mills went, he was heard to shout. It was up her nose with the rubber hose, he'd put up with her dead-loss soap and suds-for-everything ways for so long he'd live off the land if he had to, and on his pension. She wasn't getting a penny more of his money to squander on hygiene. No bloke should be expected to live like a polished piece of furniture unless they were ready to go down the rocky road to the funny farm.

He announced all this spiel at regular intervals from the top of the bandstand steps with a portable loudspeaker, after he had made his move. The news was all over town by mid-morning. Even Miss Maidstone and Athol went along to have a look and a listen to what he had to say. The house near Comfort Street, five doors away from where Athol had been brought up by Kezia and Norrie, was, as Miss Maidstone pointed out, a sodden, water-drenched write-off. Horace Mills had hosed so much water into all the rooms, up into the eaves and over the furniture that within a few days, if nothing was done, the place would most likely begin to turn into a Mould Palace, as the weather had been hot, humid and heavy for weeks. So with the help of a few locals Miss Maidstone hauled out furniture, carpets and bedding, books and clothes and curtains, and stacked it all up to dry in the front yard, before heading off down to tell Horace Mills what she'd done. He was none too pleased, he told her. His wife, whom he referred to as the Trump of the Dump, had pushed him too far. Before she left for Mitimiti she'd soaked his best shoes in a bathful of Jeyes Fluid and had put so many mothballs into his wardrobe he'd nearly been suffocated to death when he put his head in to look for a clean shirt. She'd made him hose himself down every night in the backyard for years, told everyone they knew that he had fleas and ringworm and had ruined his masculine pride, until he was nothing more than an ageing eunuch without hope. It was only the threat of fire spreading because of the long hot summer that'd stopped him from burning the whole house down instead of drenching it. From now on he was going to live in the transplanted shed his way and the Trump of the Dump could sit up and beg like an organ-grinder's monkey but he wasn't going back to her. Horace Mills told Miss Maidstone, just as he'd told the whole town, Enid could do her block when she got back and she could go bite her bum a dozen times for the next twelve months, for all he cared. She'd fussed and nagged at him about how dirty he was for long enough and he was fed up and bang had gone their marriage. He'd been losing his self-respect and manhood since he retired.

Miss Maidstone sat on the bandstand steps with Horace Mills for an hour, an arm round his shoulders, trying to calm him down after his hours of shouting, while other folk who had nothing better to do stood around like clockwork statues exercising their lips. But in the end Miss Maidstone's attempts at peacemaking were to no avail. Horace Mills shut himself into the shed and padlocked it from the inside after shouting through the keyhole that when his house-proud old lady got home he'd be there if she wanted to face him. He'd packed the shed out with supplies and reckoned he had enough food for a month, he'd been planning this escape for a month of Sundays.

Miss Maidstone's sole mission in life was still to Save Sandspit, despite the theft of the original collection of appeal money, two years before. The money never having been recovered, and Charlie Gregg along with Mrs Beryl Lamb having disappeared off the face of the earth without being caught, she continued to write letters every so often, sending them to businesses all over New Zealand and inviting them to consider the advantages of building factories or shops in the town to help boost trade. Yet though she started getting replies to her letters, no one treated them seriously and, as she told Athol, she was beginning to reckon that Sandspit Crossing might well be doomed, just as the Bidwell sisters had predicted, years ago. Yet she had to keep on fighting the battle even if folk thought she had violets growing out of her ears. Each Friday night she would link arms with Mrs Boona Gush and they would march up and down Hinemoa Parade brandishing their home-made placards, the words of which were changed every week and sometimes caused hot-headed offence. Miss Maidstone made it no secret that she thought no one gave a stuff about Sandspit's survival any longer, that was a fact, and the town's menfolk were the laziest good-for-nothing buggers in the whole civilized world, not lifting a finger to help. She even went into the hotel some nights and created a lot of disruption there, lecturing. Athol had to rescue her a few times and more than once she was verbally abused and once was given a black eye. The hotel was male territory, she was only a woman and not welcome, she was told.

Every day for hours she and Mrs Gush pored over books in the Library, while Athol sat reading with no customers, looking up new phrases that they might use for their placards. No one took much notice at all most weeks, folk in town were waiting for the announcement of the Dairy Board closure, which some still believed wouldn't actually happen because the place had stayed open for two more years than had been expected. The town had been limping along, and very little had happened to change it in the ensuing two years. Folk had just carried on with their lives. Athol had run the Library, Miss Maidstone had endlessly written letters and made preserves, which she still gave away to the needful. Past scandal had been left to rot. Summers had been hot, the winters had been wet and everyone had grown a little older but no wiser.

Athol's twenty-first birthday had come and gone without any attention being given to it. Kezia and Norrie had been away having a holiday on the Gold Coast in Australia, paid for by a mate of Norrie's who'd gone over there, after being released from prison, and winning a lot of money in a brand-new gambling casino. Kezia had arranged to telephone Athol at the Post Office on his coming-of-age day but he'd waited there for three and a half hours with no call, being entertained by Jack Lamb who talked at him about what he would do to Charlie Gregg if he ever came back to town. Jack Lamb had been quietly giving money to Raewyn Scudder, who'd changed her name back to her maiden one after her husband Charlie had left town with Jack's wife Beryl. Jack Lamb had felt responsible, and the little tyke that Raewyn had finally given birth to had had a cleft palate, a withered arm and had lived only a few months as he'd contracted a serious chest complaint – brought on, so folk said, from Charlie Gregg's bad blood. Charlie Gregg running off with Jack's wife Beryl had nearly destroyed the Scudder household. Jack had been using up all his spare cash to help them out.

During the hours that Athol waited for Kezia to telephone, Jack Lamb told him his whole life history, even the stories behind the operations he'd had, and more besides, about Beryl's years of gin-worshipping behind the counter at Young's Milk Bar and Grill. By the time Athol left the Post Office his head felt like it had been beaten for a week with a stocking full of lumpy porridge. Then after he'd been back in Comfort Street for half an hour and he and Miss Maidstone were having cocoa on her veranda, Jack Lamb came across to say that Kezia Buck had telephoned after all, but as Athol hadn't been there she'd talked to Jack instead and he'd filled her in on all the news and she'd told him that she and Norrie were thinking about settling on the Gold Coast. It was a real snazzy place with chances for making money on every street-corner, she claimed. Kezia didn't apparently say a thing about Athol having turned twenty-one, so Athol said nothing about that either. Miss Maidstone had forgotten and no one else ever remembered when his birthday was anyway. So the day he became a legal adult and was able to vote and do a lot of other things that the law had decided he was old enough to do, was no different from any other.

A few days later, however, a card arrived from Kezia and Norrie. Inside it was a silver-coloured cardboard key and a postal order for fifty pounds which Kezia had made out to Mr Norrie Buck, so Athol just put it away with the key in his tallboy drawer. He sat on his bed the day the card came and stared at the wall, listening to Miss Maidstone who was in a tip-top mood, having drawn up a dozen new placards and written five letters to General Motors in Wellington and five to Farmers in Auckland. She was out back weeding her sweet-pea patch and, despite everything, was singing 'Happy Days Are Here Again'.

The same morning that Mrs Enid Mills arrived home to find her house contents still stacked up and still soaked through in the front yard, with the plaster ceilings having collapsed in most of the rooms, the news spread about like flashes of lightning that the blokes at the Dairy Board factory were being paid off. It was the end of the road for the largest employer in Sandspit. There was more activity down Hinemoa Parade than had been seen for weeks, as the morning moved along to midday. Folk were milling about getting

themselves worked up and brains were beginning to boil. Somehow, Mrs Enid Mills, after surveying the wreckage of her life, heard
where Horace was hiding out and headed off down the Parade with
a shot-gun that she kept locked in the boot of the car she'd taken to
Mitimiti which really belonged to Horace. She was a big woman,
almost as tall as Mr Ritter with arm muscles and hips to match, and
no one had ever dared to cross her path in all the thirty years she'd
lived in Sandspit Crossing and been married to Horace, who was,
according to local dags, a bit of a DDT-soaked weed in comparison.
Mrs Enid Mills might have been a fusspot with the feather duster
but she was as tough as a full-time tank-driver. She was soon
charging along the Parade with the shot-gun tucked under her arm,
and blokes who'd been standing about munching the factory closure
news got out of her way smartly as they started expecting a *High Noon*
showdown the moment they clapped eyes on her. At the same time a
group of blokes in the Golden Hope, who'd all been employed at the
Dairy Board factory for donkey's years and had got each other riled up
from their ranting and raving and the amounts of beer they'd been
chucking back all morning, were emerging from the hotel with an
idea to barge through town across to the factory and face the bosses
there with strong words and maybe a little rough-housing.

Just as Mrs Enid Mills was passing the front of the hotel with the
shot-gun now up to her shoulder and aimed at Horace's hideaway a
few yards further along, around ten or twelve very drunk blokes
stumbled out on to the street brandishing baseball bats and billiard
cues and shouting 'Bugger the frigging bosses!' and other more
potent words in slurred voices. Mrs Mills, being a vain woman,
thought they were shouting at her. Swivelling the shot-gun round
she fired off so many cartridges from the automatic weapon that it
was like a repeat of World War II and in minutes there was
screaming and shouting and cries of agony and bodies collapsing
and by the time the police, whose office was right up the other end
of town near the Methodist-run school, were sent for, Mrs Mills
had been disarmed and was sitting in the gutter with her head in
her hands, weeping like a new-born baby, being comforted by
Raewyn Scudder's mum who'd been queueing in the butcher's and
seen it all happen through the window.

Mr Ritter had been away from the shop, down at the Millses'

backyard shed in front of the bandstand, trying to talk to Horace Mills through the padlocked door about what being a man meant. When he heard Horace's speech regarding his wife's stealing of his masculine pride, Mr Ritter was given the idea of grabbing his first convert to join his planned Chapel of Enduring Masculinity. It had been he who had disarmed Mrs Mills. He had spotted her charging down the Parade and was running towards her from the shed when the drunken factory workers emerged from the hotel and were gunned down like wild pigs. Mr Ritter had narrowly missed being shot himself by only a couple of seconds and because he'd thrown himself face down on to the pavement. He did, however, crack two of his buck-teeth. And luckily for Mrs Mills, none of the shot blokes were killed or even maimed for life, nor would they lay charges against her after the event, despite the fact that some of them got slugs in their legs and up their bums as they'd tried to get away, and in one bloke's case a couple of slugs grazed the area of his body that he reserved for his loving wife's attentions.

It caused an uproar. Half the town gathered along the Parade that night, a few hours after the gates of the Dairy Board factory were closed and the blokes who worked there had duly been paid off.

Miss Maidstone was in the thick of it, trying to organize a proper meeting. She had marshalled Mrs Boona Gush and Athol into handing out placards, some of which were a bit damp and the worse for wear, having been stored out back in her sky-blue painted lavatory for weeks. Yet when some kind of organization had been managed, no one could decide who they should march to and complain, as the bosses at the closed-down factory all lived away from Sandspit Crossing and there was no town hall they could all congregate outside. In the end a meeting was arranged to be held at the Masonic Hall the following night. Miss Maidstone volunteered to be chairman because no one else she talked at seemed to want the job, but she said they could get up a really fiery letter and the whole town could sign it and it could be packaged up and sent down to Parliament in Wellington. And when Mrs Gush spoke up and suggested that a committee could go down with the signed letter and present it in person, quite a few got whooped up over the idea. After a lot more talk everyone moved into the Golden Hope, women as well, as it was a special occasion. It was past midnight when folk packed it in and started heading off home. The night was another small triumph for Miss Maidstone. She stayed up all the rest of the night back in Comfort Street composing the letter and making endless cups of tea spiked with medicinal whisky, singing hymns so loudly that Athol didn't get a nod of sleep either.

When Athol went off to the Library the next morning, Miss Maidstone was getting herself ready for bed. She was still so full of what she had started to call the Sandspitters' Rebellion she stood on the front veranda as he left, dressed in her woollen nightie and wearing her gumboots (having been down to the beach at dawn) and holding a new placard up high which read TRIUMPH OR FAILURE, WHAT WILL YOU CHOOSE? When Athol got to the corner of Comfort Street and looked back she was still standing there waving the placard and singing 'Will Your Anchor Hold?' as loudly as her voice would allow, while Granny Barker stuck her head out of her bedroom window further along the street and yelled for Miss Maidstone to pipe down, it wasn't nine o'clock yet and she'd be along to knock her block off if Miss Maidstone didn't comply.

After the meeting at the Masonic Hall, where three blokes got into a fist fight, a couple of windows were smashed, Miss Maidstone was repeatedly shouted down when she tried to keep order and Miss Marjory Isaacs, who was a barmaid at the Golden Hope and disgracefully spoken of as a male-grinder, had an epileptic fit, life quietened down for a while. Nothing much had been achieved at the meeting. A new problem began to surface, which affected only Miss Maidstone – at first. The problem was Mr Ritter. He started sending her notes and then long letters, in which he confessed that his feelings for her had deepened and broadened over the years to the point where he worshipped the ground she walked on. Miss Maidstone was out and about even more often than ever at the time. Athol cooked their meals and kept the house tidy. Miss Maidstone was determined that she was going to get every last person in Sandspit Crossing to sign the letter to the Government, so she marched from one house to another. No one had refused to sign, but her progress was dogged by – as she put it to Athol – the buck-toothed, boar-haired, galumphing butcher. He kept leering at her from every corner and from behind every bush and she now reckoned that the only way to deal with him would be to do a Mrs Mills, get hold of a shot-gun and shoot the wretch. Every day when she arrived back at the house there'd been a new note or letter stuck under the front door. She flushed them all down the lavatory after having read the first five, which she claimed to Athol were sheer pornography and mostly misspelt.

Horace Mills had been persuaded to return to his house in Comfort Street after his wife's shoot-out and little more was happening there except Mrs Mills's taking over the restoration of their home, transporting the shed back to its rightful place in their yard and shouting at Horace while he humped furniture about and held the ladder while she checked the roof and sorted out the ceilings. She told Miss Maidstone that she wouldn't tolerate Horace's new-found Bolshiness, her squirt of a husband would be made to suffer for the rest of his natural days because of the mortification he'd put her through. She'd given him a number of Chinese burns on his stringy arms and belted him into submission with daily usage of an old pogo-stick. A marriage was a marriage. He'd never learnt who was the boss. Horace had often tried to be brave in the henhouse when the real rooster wasn't there.

Every day some families, whose bread-winners had lost their jobs at the Dairy Board factory, were packing up and leaving town. Most of them did so quietly, often after dark, and Miss Maidstone kept coming across houses that were locked up tight and a few that were even up for sale, despite the slim chances of their being sold. They were rats deserting the ship, as far as Miss Maidstone was concerned, she told Athol one night as they shared cocoa and hot buttered girdle-scones on the front veranda. She didn't know what else she could do, except to get the signed letter off quick to the Prime Minister. She'd addressed the envelope to him personally and she'd keep on writing to him until the cows came home even if he never bothered to act on her requests. She'd voted for him, after all, he was a public servant despite her having a rotten taste in her mouth every time she saw him in her mind's eye. She was acting more agitated that night than Athol had seen her for some time.

She kept getting up out of her chair and staring out into the dark, then sitting down again, only to stand up a few minutes later and pace up and down, slapping her trouser-legs and rolling cigarette after cigarette. For weeks she'd stopped rolling smokes but she'd started up again after the eighth note from Mr Ritter had been shoved under the front door. That one had been in a blue envelope with hearts drawn all over it in red ink.

When Athol said he was off to bed, Miss Maidstone told him she was going to take a walk down along the beach, which always calmed her down. She went off to look for her gumboots while Athol went off to clean his teeth and worry at a wisdom tooth that was loose.

He'd been asleep for about two hours when he heard the screaming. When he first woke up he thought he'd been dreaming, but the noise carried on. He pulled on his dressing-gown and rushed out of the house towards where the screaming was coming from and saw Miss Maidstone straight away, on her own just inside the front gate. Her hair was all over the place and her clothes were ripped and she was holding up a long stick of driftwood in the air, staring down Comfort Street towards the corner. She wasn't screaming in fear but in temper and frustration, she explained to Athol. She was ready to do murder after what she had just seen.

After he'd helped her inside and made a pot of tea she told him that she'd been idling along the water's edge admiring the moon's light on the sea when from out of nowhere Mr Ritter had appeared dressed in an oilskin and nothing else. He'd thrown himself down at her feet exposing his burgeoning privates, claiming that she was the madonna of his dreams and that he needed her more than he needed his own heart. When she tried to get away from him he chased her along and over the piles of drying seaweed to the old changing shed, where he tried to drag her inside. She had to beat him off with the piece of driftwood and ran all the way back to Comfort Street along the Parade and not one person had appeared, to help her. Mr Ritter had been right behind her all the way to the corner, shouting out things she'd never ever expected to hear from a human being and that she would never repeat even to a long-dead corpse. Just as she'd got past the old furniture factory opposite Athol's old house, he appeared again and grabbed hold of her arms and she turned round and belted him across the head repeatedly until he backed off and ran away groaning and wailing and shouting that she'd destroyed all his hope.

Athol managed to calm her down eventually and get her into bed. He stayed beside her all night, half expecting Mr Ritter to show up at the house, but it was all quiet on the Comfort Street front until mid-morning the following day. Athol stayed home from the Library and Miss Maidstone stayed in bed, after announcing that she was planning to write a long letter to her sister Ursula in Australia. She wished to be left alone, but Athol must stay in the house near her. She needed him close, he calmed her down by his just being nearby, he always had.

At noon Raewyn Scudder's dad, who suffered from angina and was one of the blokes who'd lost his job at the Dairy Board factory, turned up at the house. He'd come to see if Miss Maidstone was all right, he said, but when Athol asked him why, as he hardly knew her, Mr Scudder went beetroot and wouldn't at first say anything more except that he'd been sent. Then he reckoned that Athol should come down to Mr Ritter's shop with him and see for himself. Miss Maidstone had fallen asleep, having finished her letter to Ursula, so Athol quietly locked the front door and followed Mr Scudder along Comfort Street, and when they turned into the Parade, Athol could see a crowd of blokes standing outside the butcher's shop. When they reached it Athol wasn't able to see inside, as someone had draped sheets and blankets over the window and the door. Most of the men in the crowd had scarlet faces and wouldn't look Athol in the eye. Then in a couple of minutes, no one having explained anything, Mr Scudder suggested to Athol that he'd better have a look at what was inside the shop and held back a corner of one of the sheets. Athol shoved his head underneath. For a moment he couldn't see a thing, but as his sight grew used to the gloom he saw a sign hung up across the back of the display table which sat in the window, and the sign, in Mr Ritter's handwriting, read WILL YOU MARRY ME, MAGDALEN MAIDSTONE, I HAVE SO MUCH TO GIVE. Below the sign, spread out all over the display table, were the largest sausages Athol had ever seen, but they certainly weren't ordinary sausages. Each one of them, standing erect, had been shaped into what he knew straight away was supposed to be a male penis and to each was tied a small white cardboard label and on each label was written Miss Maidstone's name in red ink. Athol stared for a long time before he was able to pull his head out from beneath the sheet and face the waiting crowd. There were no women there, it was all right, Mr Scudder whispered to him. Any women who'd been about earlier had been herded away, though a number had already seen the display and a few had fainted, keeled over right there in the street. A search had been made for Mr Ritter, but he was nowhere to be found.

The whole town buzzed and whispered and gum-flapped in private for weeks over the affair. Mr Ritter failed to show his face, he had locked up his house and pulled down all the window blinds, leaving the keys to the shop on the counter. It was thought by most that he had simply cleared out and that the town had seen the last of him, and good riddance to bad rubbish were the words most commonly heard. The window display was cleared away smartly, the penis-shaped sausages which had been cleverly attached to sausage-meat testicles, were sealed in a sack and taken off to the town dump behind the cemetery and burnt. After a couple of days Mrs Enid Mills offered up her Horace to run the shop as no one else wanted to have anything to do with it and its future couldn't be decided on. As Mrs Mills pointed out, everyone needed meat and the walk-in freezer at the back was chocka with tasty beef cuts and chops that shouldn't be allowed to go to waste. Horace had never been a butcher before but he would do what she told him, he was a reliable sort while under her thumb.

It was decided that Miss Maidstone should never be told about Mr Ritter's obscene public proposal, but Athol had his suspicions about whether or not she knew already, because of her anger when he'd found her outside the house after being down on the beach. He reckoned privately she might have seen the display on her way home that night. She never let on, she didn't have much to say about Mr Ritter at all, but she made sure that it was Athol who went down to the butcher's shop from then on, where Horace Mills was doing his best under the watchful eye of his wife. Whatever Miss Maidstone knew or had seen or had worked out for herself, she kept to herself, without saying one word about the matter, even after Athol had overheard Granny Barker telling her a little about it out front one afternoon when he was in his bedroom with the window open. From that day on Miss Maidstone would not allow Athol to bring sausages home, and they also completely disappeared off the menu in every household in Sandspit.

It was almost a week after that when Mrs Enid Mills, having had complaints from Mr Mills that every time he went out back at the butcher's he could smell something foul, forced open the door to Mr Ritter's house. She never discovered the cause of the rotten smell but she did discover Mr Ritter's plans for his Chapel of Enduring Masculinity. All the notes, the printed talks he'd planned to give once the church was built, every handwritten directive regarding the church, along with the blueprints, were shown about town and talked about by Mrs Enid Mills once she got her hands on them, and it was only days before the whole place knew of Mr Ritter's strange and dark dreams, that he had never been the fine upstanding example of New Zealand decency everyone had believed he was. The gossip was spread as fast as a bush-fire mostly by the township women, as the subject was too touchy for blokes to deal with, after the other recent event. Once more Mr Ritter became the main topic of ear-wagging on street-corners and over tea-tables, for the written talks that Mrs Mills had found, dozens of them, were – as everyone who read them agreed – disgustingly sexual and probably illegal. Yet when Miss Maidstone heard about these latest exposures, again from Granny Barker, who came rushing along to spill the beans while Miss Maidstone and Athol were enjoying fried vegetables on toast for their tea, she couldn't stop laughing and kept on laughing for a week after. She told Athol it was a huge joke. That was something Athol hadn't expected. When Granny Barker had gone, she told Athol it was the best story she'd heard in years and the poor demented man's brain must have been turning into bug-mush for longer than even she had supposed. She'd always known he was as queer as a quacking quail under the surface. Athol never let on that he'd known about the church plans, and because Miss Maidstone was more upset about families locking up their homes and heading off down country, Mr Ritter was shoved up into the attic. For there was now genuine fear in

Miss Maidstone's heart, she confided in Athol, that life, any day now, was to change, never to be the same again. The town was slowly dying. She felt helpless to do anything more about it.

The Government eventually acknowledged the signed letter that Miss Maidstone had posted off, by sending one back to her explaining that the whole matter was certainly going to be looked into and the Prime Minister thanked her for her obvious concern. There were currently problems with a lot of small townships all over New Zealand and she wasn't to expect too much too soon, someone would be bringing it up in Session and dealing with it, she mustn't worry. The letter was a load of pig-island drivel, as far as Miss Maidstone was concerned, signed and written by some jumped-up little clerk she'd never heard of. She started writing replies addressed TO THE PRIME MINISTER ONLY every day, but as the weeks passed no one even bothered to reply or acknowledge her continued attempts to try to get something done. Folk in town told her she might just as well knock herself over the head with a cricket bat, she'd get no more satisfaction than that, for all anyone down south cared. Folk had just about had it up to their necks with trying to improve their lot and trying to hold on. The only answer was to pack up and push off to better climes, to the cities where at least chances were waiting for those with any gumption. But as Miss Maidstone told Athol, no one but her in town had really tried to fight. The only thing she could think of doing now was to organize a group like a Wild West posse, and head off down to the capital in person – to force the issue and perhaps go to the newspapers with it. That's what she just might set out to achieve. Mrs Boona Gush, whose idea it had been, was rearing to have a go, and so were a lot of other women she'd talked to, and if it was left up to them they'd kick all the men out of Parliament and women could have a go at running the country. Women couldn't make a worse job of it.

She never stopped talking to Athol for hours, every night he returned from the Library, as every night he brought home news of this family and that family who had left town hauling furniture and other possessions on trailers behind their cars and trucks. Very soon Sandspit Crossing might not be much more than a ghost town, but Miss Maidstone still held on to hope, she told Athol, there was life in Sandspit yet. All she had to come up with was some really original plan to get people riled up enough to enter the battle.

But things were slipping out of Miss Maidstone's grasp, if she'd ever had any grasp of them at all. Athol knew it and she knew it, Athol was certain of that. She'd worn out her resources and every day her face grew greyer and greyer and more strained.

Sandspit Crossing began to dry up in a deep summer heat which showed no signs of abating. There were bush-fires breaking out all over the Northland every day and every day there was not even a whiff of a sea breeze. Water was as scarce as malt whisky and at night-time Athol lay on his bed unable to move because of the humidity, listening to Miss Maidstone pacing up and down along the front veranda muttering to herself, but at least she never sang hymns out loud. She had started to stay inside the house all day with the blinds pulled down, doing little except what she referred to as getting through her thinking-cap time, until one night one of the Barker clan came running along to say that Granny Barker had died that afternoon from heat-stroke, having suffered for weeks. So Miss Maidstone emerged from the house and volunteered to help out because the Barkers weren't very good at a lot of things, and she ended up organizing the whole funeral and a get-together after, to which so many folk turned up that it became like a Masonic Hall meeting as well as a wake. Granny Barker had been one of the most popular women in Sandspit Crossing. Quite a number of folk reckoned, because Granny Barker went back in local history for decades, that it was the worst omen that could have materialized. Her death had rung the bells of doom in a very real way and folk could put a ring round that on the calendar.

It was only a few days after Granny Barker's funeral that Miss Maidstone received a cablegram from a Catholic hospital in Sydney. They were contacting her as they believed she was the sole surviving relative of a Miss Ursula Maidstone, and they had the sad task of informing her of the sudden and tragic death of her sister, who had been found at dawn the previous day locked in the arms of (an also deceased) Carmelite nun, beneath the city's Harbour Bridge. The Sydney police were treating the two deaths as suspicious. They themselves would soon be in touch by letter.

When Athol came home from the Library he found the cable-gram sitting open on the kitchen table. After he'd read it he looked out through the window and there was Miss Maidstone kneeling beside the old untouched ashes of her sculpture 'Hope Springs Eternal', her hands covering her face and her shoulders hunched forward as she wept.

Girding On the Armour

The morning Miss Maidstone made up her mind that she was going to bike down to Wellington on her Harley to confront the Prime Minister in person, with a written speech regarding Sandspit Crossing's impending doom, Mrs Boona Gush came rushing along from her house to say that her dead husband had come back to her during the night. He'd dragged her out by the roots of her hair into the backyard and made wild passionate love to her on the dew-drenched grass. She even showed Miss Maidstone and Athol her damp, badly stained nightie. Athol had just made breakfast from left-over doughboys he'd heated up in the oven.

Mrs Gush was in such a state it took Miss Maidstone a couple of hours to calm her down, to convince her that she'd probably just had a horrible nightmare and had walked in her sleep. Though she couldn't explain the stained nightie, Miss Maidstone believed Mrs Gush had been subconsciously affected by the memory of Mrs Kathleen McCauley, who'd thought her dead husband had returned to haunt her by letter and who had ended up dying in a mental hospital, and surely Mrs Gush was made of sterner stuff than that.

In the end Mrs Gush pulled herself together after having a cry. She went home to hand-wash her living-room curtains which always took her mind off brain worries and, as she admitted, blew away the cobwebs.

Mrs Boona Gush had lost both her husband Endel and her daughter Elaine within two weeks of one another, a decade ago. Since their deaths – Endel Gush having kicked the bucket from tuberculosis and Elaine having been run over and killed by a tractor when the farmer driving it along the Parade had been drinking for the previous five hours – Mrs Gush had for years lived as a hermit. In her house on Comfort Street, or close to it, she had created a mausoleum with the blinds pulled down and had not seen the light of day for years. She was always dressed in black, with a face to welcome the undertaker, and it wasn't until Miss Maidstone had barged in one day and brought Mrs Gush out into the bosom of society that a lot of folk in town remembered that she was still alive.

Sandspit Crossing was now half empty and a sad sack of a place. Six months had passed since the closing of the Dairy Board factory. Families had left town in hordes, determined never to come back. Life was holding on by a thread. On the surface the streets didn't look all that much different from what they had looked like back when Athol had been a teenager, just less people on them, more weeds on the pavements and no one ever came across a lost sixpence in the gutter any longer. The streets were quieter at night. Few strangers were ever spotted. Anyone passing through had usually taken a wrong turning and soon corrected their mistake. Local farmers had deserted the town completely. They had begun buying supplies from Donnelly's Crossing, or drove down to Kaihu. Many families that were left were living off the Government on Social Security while they sorted out their futures and fought apathy. The local police station, which had been only small, was now closed, the two good blokes who'd worked there transferred to Dargaville headquarters, which was to police the town from then on. The Methodist-run school had also been shut down and any children still in Sandspit were sent off out of town on the same bus that Athol had gone to school on, years before.

It was all vertical drinking at the Golden Hope every night for
the out-of-work left-overs while the town was up dung-creek in
leaky gumboots, Miss Maidstone kept telling Athol over the breakfast table. She was overwhelmed by all the changes. The changes
called for drastic action, which was why she planned to bike down
to Wellington in a last bid. The Prime Minister had to listen and do
something, even if he *was* a septic pot-stirrer who went off pop only
when hard times hit the rich. No one gave a jigger of sympathy for
ordinary country folk. It was townies this and townies that all the
way along the lifeline, as far as politicians were concerned. Even
the farmers had been on a bad trot for years. The new full-of-
promise decade which the Government were going on and on about
in tinsel tones was nothing more than one more trip around the
gasworks and the ning-nongs who were pretending to run the
country were as useless as warts on the nose.

Kezia and Norrie Buck had settled on the Gold Coast in Australia. Kezia had written to Athol saying that they had no hankering
to return to New Zealand. Norrie had a taste for the big time now
and they both had a real chance to get rich quick, if all went
according to plan. She'd be sending some money soon to Athol if
he intended to stay put. Kezia was opening a modern beauty parlour
and Norrie was involved in a scheme to produce electric motor
launches, which he reckoned would make them millionaires before
too long, despite their being treated like they were a dead loss
because they came from New Zealand.

Miss Maidstone had also received a letter, from Mr Ritter. She
didn't know where it'd been sent from as the postmark was smudged
and there was no return address inside. It told her in no uncertain
terms that Magdalen Maidstone would always be the rainbow-
tinted flower garden of Mr Ritter's bruised heart, that despite all his
dreams having been shattered he held her to him in spirit. One day
he might return, to carry her away to paradise.

The letter was written on pink paper with roses printed round its
edges. As Miss Maidstone told Athol after she'd read it, his choice
of words was enough to make her want to bring up all the meals
she'd eaten in the last week, to say nothing of the atrocious spelling
and the broken hearts he'd drawn after his signature. She hoped

she'd seen the last of Mr Reginald Wallace Ritter, as he'd signed his piece of insulting tripe. It was just as well he wasn't within reach, she'd be tempted to crack his jaw in a dozen places. At least now she could get about town without having to put up with his yellowing buck-teeth being exposed to her several times a day – or anything else for that matter.

For a few weeks, before they were bussed off out of town to learn their ABCs, Miss Maidstone had thrown herself into organizing school lessons in her backyard for – as she put it – the abandoned tiny folk of Sandspit Crossing. She knocked up a few desks from more planks she and Athol filched from the now derelict and half-collapsed furniture factory, somehow found a child's blackboard and chalks, with Athol providing books from the Library. The Library was also now threatened with closure. Athol had received two circulars recently to tell him that, as the future to Sandspit was hanging in the balance, he might soon have to seek employment elsewhere. The Library wouldn't be viable if any more folk decided to leave town.

Miss Maidstone's School of Learning lasted for two days. It wasn't a complete failure. She managed to read aloud some stories of far-away lands but lost control when the five children all of school age grew bored and went rampaging through the house one morning. She'd left them to do sums and drawings while she took Athol the packed lunch he'd left behind. One child cracked a window in the living-room, managed to knock down and smash some of her best crockery, and one little terror called Noggy Noakes, who'd eaten three green apples and kept poking his tongue out and farting every time she smiled at him, chucked up all over her bed and had to be rushed off to hospital in Dargaville. After that Miss Maidstone lost interest. The children were sent to a proper school outside town by bus. She hadn't really wanted to try her hand at educating, she explained to Athol after the makeshift school was abandoned. She'd just thought it her duty. She'd been hoping it might lead to better things. She'd had an idea for a while to open up an educational establishment and name it after her poor dead sister, for whom she still grieved and always would. But the idea had begun to seem in bad taste after a while. The children had less manners than monkeys in a zoo because their parents were

Philistines without much gumption for advancement themselves. The town had been reduced to almost nothing but no-hopers in the last six months, though that hadn't quashed her reasons for trying to save it.

Miss Maidstone had heard from the Sydney police, asking for details about Ursula, because of her death. She sent a fifteen-page letter in return, telling them everything she could remember about Ursula's life. She sent money for a funeral, money for a wreath, but didn't want to go over to Australia for the service. The Catholic Church had taken Ursula back into its bosom and buried her, along with the Carmelite nun. A verdict of death by misadventure was recorded at an inquest and three weeks later a priest called Father Humphrey Macdougall wrote to say that Ursula was at peace now, Miss Maidstone must not think that her beloved sister had been neglected. She had been well known in the district and would now forever be in the arms of Jesus, who forgave all. Nothing was ever explained regarding the circumstances of Ursula's death. Miss Maidstone confessed to Athol that it might be best not to inquire. For two weeks she carried the letter around with her in a pocket, until one day Athol saw it propped up on the mantel. Then it disappeared. Miss Maidstone never talked of Ursula again, but beside her bed from that day forward stood a framed photograph of her and Ursula as children, holding hands and smiling, beneath a cabbage tree on the beach at Knuckle Point.

After Miss Maidstone had studied a map for three days and worked out a bike-route down to the capital as well as a list of things she wanted to say in a speech when she came face to face with the main man on top of the political dunghill, Mrs Gush, who'd been told to pull on her own thinking-cap, came up with the idea of hiring a bus. She and Athol and Miss Maidstone had just finished lunch together. It was Saturday. Athol had cooked savoury mince on toast and lime jelly.

The town could chip in, Mrs Gush reckoned, and hire a Newman's coach which a delegation of women could travel in all the way down to Parliament Buildings in Wellington and park outside, taking with them the placards she and Miss Maidstone had come up with, and even more if they got ideas from other local brains. Once there they could sit it out and sling the mustard until they got satisfaction.

As soon as Mrs Gush's lips were shut Miss Maidstone jumped up and down on the kitchen floor and yelled out 'Eureka' a couple of times and told Mrs Gush after hugging her that with such ideas they could save the world, let alone their small backblocks settlement the blowflies were deserting. From then on it was whoopee for the winterless north, Miss Maidstone was determined to rescue the day, the idea would make Saving Sandspit as smooth as spreading mustard. If the Prime Minister knew that a group of country ladies were converging on his male kingdom he'd be bound to sit up and take notes, even if it was only out of politeness. Within a few hours she had organized Mrs Gush into shunting around town with a tin bucket for donations and a new placard explaining the whole plan, while Miss Maidstone wrote lists of what a dozen women would need on such a trip, what clothes should be worn to make a good impression, and even who should be in the delegation. There were a number of women still living in Sandspit, she explained to Athol, who would be as useless as a whistle without a pea when it came to diplomatic dung-chucking. The choice of who should go on the coach would be hard yacker. But she felt in her water that it was the best idea yet. Why she hadn't come up with it herself was beyond reach. Mrs Boona Gush wasn't exactly university material and her long period of mourning had made her act a bit queer sometimes, even when it wasn't a full moon.

It had been raining off and on for weeks. A long, wet, cold winter was forecast. Yet that prospect didn't dampen Miss Maidstone during those weeks, she was overflowing with energy and ideas and plans as if it was the beginning of spring. Already there'd been reports of flooding up north. Further south sheep and cattle had been lost in raging rivers and low-lying areas inland had become so bogged down that a few farms with all their livestock had been shifted to higher ground. Every morning there were heavy skies and a bitter wind blowing through town. Miss Maidstone had even given up on her dawn walks down to the beach.

The roof of the Library had sprung half a dozen leaks. Athol spent most of his days in there emptying full buckets down the lavatory and mopping the floor, shifting all the shelves once he'd taken down the books, so there'd be no damage. The Majestic Picture Theatre flooded one night, with so many streams of water pouring down through the roof and splashing from the exposed rafters that the latest Esther Williams picture, which had been kept over for two weeks as folk wanted to see it again, took on a whole new atmosphere and meaning.

'If You Don't Help Yourself, Nobody Else Will' was Miss Maidstone's phrase of the day as the idea to hire a Newman's coach began to grab attention and loosen tongues all across town. She had ideas to have the saying painted in huge letters along both sides of the coach, with all the side-windows painted over in white and other slogans painted there in bright green and gold. But in the end Newman's Coaches, whom she wrote to, turned down her request for a free coach. They couldn't agree to the paint-job idea. Yet there came a strong promise of an old bus which was owned and once operated for transporting crates of slaughtered chooks down to Whangarei by Raewyn Scudder's Uncle Frodo up in Awanui. He offered to drive the bus down to Sandspit a week or more before the day Miss Maidstone planned to set out with her band of hopeful handmaidens. Jack Lamb had offered tins of paint. Mrs Enid Mills offered up Horace for anything Miss Maidstone might like to use him for. Pretty soon ideas and other offers were pouring in, with a little money and tins of food, but when Jack Lamb added to his offer of paint a few dozen sausages which he said he'd cook and pack up himself, Miss Maidstone made it clear she wasn't interested in that. The Sandspit delegation, however, was really on the go. Once again Miss Maidstone was in the limelight. Folk were knocking on her door at all hours with offers of picnic baskets and blankets and even a small searchlight run on a battery which could be bolted on to the roof of the bus so it could be shone into the windows of Parliament Buildings – to wake up, the dag who'd offered it added, the sleeping dead.

There were quite a few in town who reckoned it was useless throwing even a bunch of women at the mercy of the Government. Mad-dogging politicians was simply asking for a knock-back. The women would still be sitting on their jumbos in the coach half-way through to the next century before anything was done except for a lot of political ear-wagging and empty promises. That was all politicians did and ever would do. It was up to Sandspitters themselves to save the place if they really wanted it saved. Miss Maidstone heard the argument every time she walked about with her donation bucket and it made her wild. She told Athol that it was all just talk-mongering, and at least she and her ladies were taking action. They'd win through in the end, she had faith and hope and didn't mind what kind of charity was handed out so long as it saved the township and meant that she could go on living where her soul had roots until her heavenly number was called.

Athol received another letter from Kezia, telling him that she was hacked off with the Gold Coast. The whole area was a dead loss. She and Norrie had made a lot of money and it was all gathering nuts in the bank, but the town they lived in was a dead-loss town and the so-called mates Norrie had been drinking with were nothing but dead-loss con-artists and each one tried to rip him off with every second breath. They'd met a truly bonzer bloke from California who claimed he could get them into America through the back door, where they stood a better chance of winning the sort of life they craved. He was making inquiries on their behalf. Would Athol like to go across to live in America with her and Norrie? She really missed her only son and was dead certain he would love the United States. Randy Delaney, their new mate who had been born in Texas and was a handsome brute, was certainly good and keen to take them across the water in his luxury yacht. She and Norrie were moving further up the coast to where Randy lived. He'd booked them into an American-style trailer park until they found a proper house. Norrie was working for Randy's company. Randy Delaney was an Italian-American and had his own business empire which had fingers in pies all over the world and an office in New York. No one talked about what he actually did, though he had all sorts working for him and had five bodyguards. He'd told Kezia he could get Athol a job too.

The letter went on for five pages but didn't mean a great deal to Athol after he'd read it a few times. Kezia and Norrie seemed to be moving further and further away in miles as they were from his life and he wondered if he would ever see them again. Miss Maidstone hardly ever mentioned them except to ask if they were all right when Kezia's letters arrived. It felt to Athol sometimes as if he had lived with Miss Maidstone all his life and would be living with her for the rest of it. He sat down and wrote to Kezia that he didn't think he wanted to go to America, but that she and Norrie must go if they had the chance. There was nothing stopping them.

Business in Sandspit carried on more or less as usual despite everything. Jack Lamb juggled the running of the Post Office with Young's Milk Bar and Grill, helped out by Raewyn Scudder and her mum most days. The Four Square grocery had changed hands again. It wasn't doing very good trade but it was the only place in town where folk could get credit. Somehow life went along almost as if there was no hardship at all, despite most folk moaning about how broke they were. A few cracked on that there were more Social Security payments coming into town than into the whole of North-land.

Rain carried on falling at least five days a week and reports of flooding were on the radio news every day. The whole country was awash and threatened by being turned into a bog. There wasn't even an end to the deluge in sight, according to the experts. It was Noah-time all over again.

The bus which had been driven down from Awanui by Raewyn Scudder's Uncle Frodo and lent to Miss Maidstone, had been parked in front of her house and a huge tarpaulin held up by old telegraph-poles had been keeping it dry. Every morning Miss Maidstone and Mrs Gush and anyone else around who was handy with a paintbrush was out there in gumboots and oilskins transforming it into the strangest-looking vehicle that Athol had ever seen. Miss Maidstone wanted the bus to be noticed, as it made its way down-country for the confrontation in Wellington. She lived and breathed the bus, talked of nothing else during those weeks before she and the other women were to set out. There were ten Sandspit women chosen by vote for the delegation, including Miss Maidstone and Mrs Gush, who was to be the driver. It was to be Miss Maidstone's job to keep the other women cheered up and geared up to face what she reckoned was to be a battle with the bigwigs. They'd really have to pull out all the stops once they were down there, to make themselves heard and show they meant business.

The bus was painted white all over, with yellow windows.

Slogans were painted on the roof in red and green. Balloons, placards and a shallow-cut orange-box from which fireworks were to be
let off were all organized and ready, to be attached around the edges
of the roof and on the bonnet, where a sign was to hang that read
WOMEN OF THE WORLD UNITE! WELLINGTON OR BUST!
There was no point, Miss Maidstone explained to the perplexed,
in just taking down an ordinary-looking bus, even if this one was older
than Moses and a bit of a rust-bucket underneath the paint. The
whole idea was to grab attention from the word go and that was
what she intended to do. She'd been practising with the portable
loudspeaker Horace Mills had lent her, standing in the backyard
yelling through it, even in the falling rain. Athol would come
home from the Library and above the hiss of the downpour he
would hear her voice bellowing out 'We want recognition!' or 'We
might be from the scrub but we won't take the rub!' and other
expressions which she and Mrs Gush had written down into a
notebook.

One afternoon a group of concerned old male codgers came into
the Library to tell Athol they thought Miss Maidstone was losing
control, that she was as likely to be taken seriously with her joke of
a bus as would be a talking tree tomato. The Government weren't
going to get off their fat behinds for a place that was half dead
anyway. Everyone knew Miss Maidstone was a hard shot and a good
sort but, just as it was said about over-indulging in booze, 'The hand
that lifts the cup of cheer, should not be used to shift the gears.'
Miss Maidstone was biting off more than she could chew. As a
woman she might take a long fall into dog-poop if she wasn't
careful. Every bloke in town was grateful for what she was organizing but city folk were gorsepockets when it came to helping, as
mean as Fagins. When the bus turned up on the Wellington streets
the ladies would get laughed off into the middle of next week by
cold-hearted townies.

After that, Athol had so many come in to tell him privately their
little homilies. He didn't know if he should say anything about it to
Miss Maidstone or not. She was crammed full of hope and energy
and was out beside the bus slapping on the paint and polishing the
leather seats at dawn most mornings, charging about town with the
donation bucket and walking for miles in the rain to outlying farms

collecting a shilling here and two bob there or a promise from the penniless. He didn't have the heart to let on about those talking behind her back and wondering about her sanity. He said nothing and just hoped for the best, like the folk who were involved and helping out felt. The opinion amongst them was high that Miss Maidstone's plan might change life as Sandspitters currently knew it.

A couple of days before the delegation send-off, after the bus had finished being decorated and the rain had unexpectedly eased, an articulated truck hauling a wheeled mobile crane was seen heading into town, just after sunrise. A lot of folk at first reckoned it was something Miss Maidstone had held up her sleeve to do with the trip to Wellington, but it was soon known that the convoy was coming to take away every wooden plank and window-frame of Raeleen Cressell's bach behind the cemetery. The Icon's followers had bought a section of land in the Wellington hills where the famous dead sculptress's bach was to be transported and transformed into a National Treasure and a women's museum, with the help of a huge Government grant.

None of the Apostles who'd asked Miss Maidstone to join their last vigil had contacted her to let her know they were turning up, that they had been given the grant, but the news wasn't long in reaching Comfort Street. Miss Maidstone pulled on her gumboots and her oilskin and told Athol they were to get over to the bach straight away so she could find out the true facts. Athol had been baking raisin bread and bran biscuits in the oven at the time and didn't want to leave them, but Miss Maidstone was adamant. With Athol right behind her she barged across the boggy paddocks, taking a short cut, and by the time she reached the Cressell land, steel ropes were already being attached to the bach from the crane so it could be lifted on to the truck. Mrs Kingston-Smith and Mrs Dorothy Dakota were there and appeared to be in charge of the proceedings. Along with a few hefty Maori and Pakeha blokes, they were wearing oilskin boiler suits with motor-bike crash-helmets on their heads, shouting directions and rushing to and fro, and at first neither of them took any notice of Miss Maidstone's and Athol's arrival. A huge crowd of local folk were already standing about staring, with Mrs Enid Mills yelling instructions at her husband Horace whom she'd taken across to offer a hand. It wasn't until the whole bach had been carefully raised into the air away from its makeshift foundations that Miss Maidstone collared Mrs Kingston-Smith and asked why she hadn't been informed of the whole matter. She was, after all, supposed to be one of the ten Raeleen Cressell Apostles, and no one at all in Sandspit had been informed, or even asked, about the removal.

Heavy rain had begun to fall again by then. Though the wind had dropped, it was colder than it had been for weeks. Whatever Mrs Kingston-Smith shouted to Miss Maidstone in reply above the sound of the rain got her so worked up and wild that they were shouting at each other, getting more and more agitated for quite a time until for some reason the set-to led to blows. Before anyone noticed what was developing, Miss Maidstone and Mrs Kingston-Smith were at each other's throats then, bashing out with their fists, and when one of the Maori blokes ran across the mud to see if he could sort it out, Mrs Dorothy Dakota let fly at him before leaping on to Miss Maidstone because of something she had yelled at her. Minutes later a few locals came to Miss Maidstone's aid, no one really knowing how the fight had begun or why it was happening but realizing that there was a serious fight going on and that Miss Maidstone appeared to be on the receiving end of it. Things somehow got out of control after that. Very soon there were about eight or ten women and blokes, including Horace Mills and Jack Lamb, slugging each other and wrestling in the mud, fists and legs were flying about and bodies were sliding all over the show and from where Athol was standing he couldn't tell who was who and why Mrs Dorothy Dakota had Miss Maidstone in a leg-lock on the ground beating her across the bottom with a leather belt she'd removed from the waist of her boiler suit. When Mrs Kingston-Smith managed to grab hold of Miss Maidstone by the hair and started to drag her across the mud towards where the mobile crane was parked, Athol ran across and shoved Mrs Kingston-Smith in the back with both hands, knocking off her crash-helmet. Then he grabbed her arms, yelling at her to let go, which she did, only to turn and sock Athol in the jaw with one of her freed fists, sending him flat on his back into some gorse bush. Meanwhile Jack Lamb had rushed forward and grabbed Mrs Dakota's waist and was shouting for everyone to calm down. Mrs Dakota bit him on the hand and followed that up with a back-kick into the groin which was so well aimed that after it was all over he was hardly able to walk more than a few steps and had to wear a truss for six weeks.

The fight lasted for more than twenty minutes, mostly going on in the mud below the dangling bach, which was swinging wildly on its steel ropes fifteen feet in the air above the battling bodies. When the fighting did stop, folk stood about staring at each other in amazement and shock, still not knowing how on earth it had started or why and there was a great deal of confusion and argument. Eventually someone got all those involved to agree to retreat to the hotel. They could dry off in there and sort anything out that needed to be sorted.

It was hours later and after some kind of a truce had been called that the bach was lowered down on to the truck and tied securely with rope. Half the town turned out to watch, despite the rain still bucketing down. An agreement of sorts had been reached inside the hotel, though Miss Maidstone was still dead set against the whole idea of letting the bach be taken away. She didn't think the great sculptress's home should be moved at all, official museum or not. There'd been a great deal of shouting and abuse and a near-return to fists before the matter was uneasily sorted. Most folk in town didn't mind about the removal, they couldn't understand Miss Maidstone's fury despite defending her, and reasoned that it was up to Raeleen Cressell's followers and the Government who had got involved to do whatever they wanted with the bach. The crumbling old shack wasn't worth a brass razoo and had been an eyesore for years, the area where it had sat was prime land and could be sold off for a new factory if they could get an offer. It wasn't as if Raeleen Cressell had been buried locally. If a museum was being planned down in the capital then good luck to them, everyone had to have a fair go at things. A dead sculptress didn't mean a great deal to country folk when half of them were out of work, down in the doldrums and just plain broke.

What caused Miss Maidstone's fury to rise to the ceiling was that Mrs Kingston-Smith denied ever having suggested that Miss Maidstone be an Apostle, and when that was revealed it almost came to

murderous blows between the two. But in the end Miss Maidstone
had no choice but to back off after all the arguments. She stood
silently with a livid face while last-minute details were agreed to
and everyone except her was satisfied that the removal was legal
and above board.

Just before the day had completely gone into night townsfolk
stood about watching outside the hotel as if it was a real parade
down the main street, as the low-on-the-ground truck was manoeuvred slowly along, heading out of town towards the south-bound
State Highway. Miss Maidstone stared, holding on to Athol's arm,
his hand crushed to her breast, her face so pale that Athol was
worried she might faint. Once the convoy had passed out of sight,
past the empty police station and turning right into Rideout Road
to the highway, Miss Maidstone moved into the middle of Hinemoa Parade and stood there alone, everyone else except Athol
having gone back into the hotel which had been kept open for the
occasion. She wouldn't speak to Athol. She wouldn't speak to
anyone at all, despite Mrs Gush making attempts at offering sympathy and Mrs Enid Mills bringing out a jug of sweet hot tea. After
about half an hour Miss Maidstone started walking slowly away
along the middle of the Parade, not looking to her left or right, her
head lowered. Athol followed her all the way back to the house.
When they reached the grass verge on which sat the decorated bus
she stood for a long time staring at it, not moving, while Athol
went inside to change into dry clothes. It had been the goofiest day
he had been through for a long while.

The following morning, hours before dawn, Miss Maidstone was
up and about and woke Athol to tell him that today was the day,
she wanted him to get dressed and hot-foot it to every house
involved to tell them that the bus was leaving for Wellington in
two hours. If the delegated women weren't ready it'd be their bad
luck, it was now or never and she was ready to gird her loins and go
fight the battle. She didn't say one word about the events of the day
before, after she'd hauled Athol out of bed and he'd made breakfast.
She ate two bowls of porridge, three slices of doorstop toast and a
peeled apple standing at the kitchen sink, staring through the
window. By the time Athol had been out to warn all the women
and had rushed back to the house, Miss Maidstone had taken down

the tarpaulin sheltering the bus and it was parked out in the middle of Comfort Street in thin sunlight, covered with hand-made streamers, placards and the balloons Miss Maidstone told Athol she'd been up half the night filling with her lung-power. She had Mrs Gush already sitting in the driver's seat revving up the cold engine. Mrs Gush was trying to sing the words of 'Hark! 'Tis the Clarion' which Miss Maidstone had taught her and was the theme song for the trip, to be sung all along the road down to Wellington – she'd printed up copies of the hymn on the Library Gestetner.

So just as Mrs Gush was belting out 'Banners are waving, swords gleaming bright, gird on the heavy armour', the rest of the women, who included Raewyn Scudder and her mum, Mrs Enid Mills, Dolly McArthur, a few of the Barker clan, along with a cousin of the wife of Bulldog-Bill Cutty who now ran the Four Square grocery, all appeared along Comfort Street lumbered with baskets of food, umbrellas and cricket bats for protection. Miss Maidstone rushed here and there organizing, calling out encouragement and acting so cheerful and in control that Athol, watching from the front veranda, reckoned she'd forgotten all about having lost yesterday's battle to protect the removal of the Icon's bach. He didn't know what to say to her about it when she'd woken him up but she hadn't encouraged him to say anything, all the way through breakfast.

By the time the bus was ready to set off, dozens of families, and children who weren't at school, were lined up like royalty-watchers along Comfort Street. Miss Maidstone, dressed in her oilskin buttoned to the neck, proper boots she'd spent hours polishing and on her head her best straw hat, was standing on top of the bus waving a paper New Zealand flag and smiling. She'd hugged Athol goodbye as quickly as she'd said goodbye to others who'd come along to see the women leave. Before Athol was able to take it all in the bus was coughing and backfiring its way down the street towards the corner, children trying to chase after it to grab at the dozens of balloons hanging down from its roof, Miss Maidstone still managing to balance herself on top of the roof by holding on to the metal frame Jack Lamb had constructed, which held the searchlight she was planning to use. The other women, all dressed up to the nines, were waving from the opened windows and yelling out to husbands and family.

As folk said after the bus had gone out of sight, it sure made the taking away of Raeleen Cressell's bach look crummy, the Sandspit delegation bus had been the best sight in town for months and it was all due to Miss Maidstone, she deserved a medal for what she was trying to do. Not one person mentioned the fist fight of the day before and the general knowledge that it'd been Miss Maidstone who had supposedly started it. As the bus reached the end of Comfort Street and started to turn the corner, a huge cheer went up while rain suddenly began to plummet down more heavily than before out of a black sky. In moments the street was deserted, everyone along it fleeing for cover. Athol was invited by Horace Mills, now that his wife was out of earshot, to go and have a few free beers at the Golden Hope. As Horace told him – while the women were away making idiots of themselves, the men of the town could act normal and start having a good time – quite a few were planning a fair dinkum booze-up all that night and who'd blame them in the circumstances? The women would do as good a job as they could down in the big smoke and every bloke in the hotel would be cheering them on. It'd been ladies-choice to go.

It was two days before anyone heard what happened after that. The first Athol knew about it was spotting the decorated bus being hauled back into town behind a tow-truck along Hinemoa Parade, just as he was coming out of the Library, having locked up for the day. Horace Mills and Raewyn Scudder's Uncle Frodo were planning to take him out deep-sea fishing in Frodo's dinghy. The rain had cleared up.

There was no one inside the bus. It was a total wreck, sides buckled inward and most of the painted-over windows smashed, with two of its wheels missing and a gaping hole in the roof.

A huge crowd gathered in minutes along Hinemoa Parade once the news had spread over town. The bus had managed to reach the outskirts of Babylon, so the story went from the tow-truck driver who was related to the Barkers and knew everyone. When the accident had happened, it was thought that Miss Maidstone had been driving, and because of the heavy rain, she hadn't seen what was up front. The Raeleen Cressell bach, still intact and standing low on the back of the articulated truck which had broken down, had been parked along the side of the road beside the river, but the bus had somehow skidded across the tarmac and slammed straight into the rear of the bach without any warning to anyone. The ancient rattletrap had been travelling at great speed – the impact had shattered the bach despite its being covered with tarpaulin, so it had collapsed somehow, come loose from its ropes and fallen sideways into the overflowing Kaihu river which'd been a raging torrent for days. The bach had been washed away before anyone could do a thing to save it. The bus had followed, driving straight into the river, and it was hours before the women trapped inside were brought out after a hole in the roof was blow-torched, the bus having wedged itself on hidden rocks below the water-level, preventing it too being washed away. The whole accident had been witnessed by a local farmer out searching for a couple of his prize-winning sows who'd escaped from their paddock through a rickety fence.

No one had been killed, though there were multiple injuries. Raewyn Scudder, who again was pregnant, this time by some unknown male from out of town, had suffered a miscarriage. Miss Maidstone had been bruised badly and had damaged her kneecaps but they weren't broken, Athol was told. No one received any really serious injuries at all, as far as the tow-truck driver knew, and he reckoned it was a true miracle. The women were all suffering from shock and exposure though and were now in Dargaville Hospital. No one from the articulated truck had been present at the time of the crash. The truck had broken down the day before, and Mrs Kingston-Smith along with her cohorts were sleeping in a nearby motel at the time the crash occurred – they were waiting for a special engine part to be sent up from Auckland. The Sandspit bus was a wreck, it was of no more value now than scrap metal, there'd been something seriously wrong with its steering and it should never have been allowed on the road, especially with a bunch of inexperienced women, so the police had stated. No one was to blame, except perhaps for Raewyn Scudder's Uncle Frodo for having supplied the bus in the first place. The whole business had been a near-fatal disaster. To top it all, the Dargaville police were dealing with a formal accusation from Mrs Kingston-Smith that Miss Maidstone had deliberately set out to destroy the New Zealand

Icon's home. The serious charges which had been laid against her might mean that Miss Maidstone could end up in the middle of a court case, and, it was feared, in the midst of a massive national scandal.

After the Ghoul Had Gone

It was Mrs Dolly McArthur's visiting sister Mysie Eskett who first spotted a Living Spectre one night, after she'd gone out front to hurl one of Arthur McArthur's boots at a couple of fighting tom-cats. She was down from Diggers Valley for a visit, leaving her husband to fend for himself, in an effort to persuade Mr and Mrs McArthur to move up to the valley to live with her and Godley Eskett, who was a well-known sheep-dip manufacturer. Opening the front door of the McArthur house on Anzac Avenue just before midnight, she was bending down trying to see where the cats were hiding when she looked up and saw instead the dark shape of a tall man lurking beside a telegraph-pole on the other side of the street. Before she could cry out, the figure had opened up the rubber mack he was wearing and exposed to her the most skeletal set of naked bones and flesh she'd ever seen since she'd worked in a male geriatric ward at a Wellington hospital during the last war. She'd shrieked like a banshee then, for Arthur McArthur, and clapped her eyes shut before collapsing in a faint, but by the time Arthur had pulled up his trousers and hurried out from where he'd been sitting on the lavatory reading a copy of *Mechanics Illustrated*, the corpse-like figure had gone. After that night Mrs Eskett headed home as fast as she could arrange it, not having accomplished a thing. It wasn't to be too long before the cadaverous peril who became known as The Ghoul held the whole town in its gruesome grip.

Miss Maidstone, along with Mrs Boona Gush and all the other women from the Babylon bus wreck, had been safely back in their homes from Dargaville Hospital for five months and the weather had turned. Instead of heaving down rain, the daily sky was now the deepest shade of blue that anyone living could remember and the sun was so hot you could have fried a dozen eggs on the roof of anyone's tinder-dry house before noon and topped that off with some saveloys or chops for tea. Sandspit Crossing might be about to be gripped by a nasty underweight sexo, but the whole of the Northland was already in the clutches of one of the worst droughts ever recorded, and it wasn't even close to Christmas. The unnatural, fast-changing weather over the last year had been a subject everyone had ear-wagged about constantly until along came the even more abnormal Ghoul to take minds off the climate and create chaos. And what was to follow afterwards was to change everyone's lives for evermore.

The Raeleen Cressell affair had thundered across the pages of most New Zealand newspapers and was discussed by concerned brains on the radio. For quite a few weeks Miss Maidstone became a known name throughout the country. Once it was all over and the collection money had been handed back (every last penny having been saved), she started to get so many letters delivered to her letter-box out front that she paid Jack Lamb to make her a larger one painted white with her name on it in gold-coloured lettering as well as the number of the street. After all the letters she'd written to the many so-called friends she'd made on her travels in younger days which had brought almost no replies, she was now up half the night surrounded by dozens of How are you, now you're all rights to reply to, and with her trusty fountain-pen had used up so many writing-pads and envelopes that Arthur McArthur who looked after stationery over the counter in the General Goods was ordering twice as much as he could ever recall having ordered in thirty years.

The threatened court case from Mrs Kingston-Smith hadn't come about. The Raeleen Cressell Apostle had withdrawn her accusations and pushed off overseas to Indo-China, where Cressell followers were supposed to be legion. As Miss Maidstone told Athol, the woman had been the sort who wanted the penny and the bun too, she thought she was clever but her feet stank like everyone else's. The whole group of them could put the hard word on for the next century but no one could prove she'd deliberately crashed that bus. She hadn't, anyway. She'd just not seen the parked bach because of the rain and had lost control of the steering. It'd been the last thing she'd wanted, to destroy the New Zealand Icon's bach. She was as devastated as everyone else. There'd never been enough cultural history in New Zealand as it was. Now there was even less.

For a few weeks there were so many walking-sticks being used along Sandspit streets after the delegation of women had been ambulanced back to their homes that it could have been a threat to the national forests if it had gone on for much longer. A lot of the women had suffered multiple leg injuries of varying kinds in the crash. Miss Maidstone's kneecaps were still troubling her. The remedy she'd been told to use along with the other women was slow walking with the aid of a stout stick or even two and to keep her legs up when she sat down. There'd been badly bruised shins, lacerated thighs, twisted ligaments and swollen ankles in almost every street around town. Mrs Gush had had little to contend with except bad bruising on her bottom, for she'd been one of the fortunate. Raewyn Scudder's mum, having recovered from the shock of her daughter's miscarriage, developed complications and three weeks after the accident had to have her left foot sawn off and she was now, along with her husband and Raewyn, down in Wellington being treated. She wrote to Miss Maidstone saying that she didn't think they would be coming back to Sandspit Crossing. She was being fitted with the best false foot New Zealand could produce, Mr Scudder having made sure of that, while they stayed with her Exclusive Brethren sister in Cashmere.

No one in town had blamed Miss Maidstone for the accident, and none of the newspaper stories accused her of having been solely responsible. There was a certain amount of guarded sympathy for her predicament which was why, according to her, she had started to get so many letters.

One woman called Miss Flora Coote wrote to tell her that she was certain to be interested in the fact that the name Maidstone came from a French word Maidstus, which was a town in Europe from where the persecuted Hoganellas had fled to England, and if Miss Maidstone's ancestors were indeed of Old Country stock from which most New Zealand folk had originated, then she'd descended from a line of very tough and resilient females and should take heart over that. Miss Coote admired the way Miss Maidstone had coped with the business of having her photograph in the newspapers and the fact that she'd never chosen to marry. Men were the nastiest forms of life she could think of on God's earth. She'd always kept dogs (neutered bitches, of course) and swore by them as companions.

There were a few letters filled with hate, one accusing her of being filled with Satan and evil, some thanking her without explaining what for, and one morning there arrived a copy of the Bible from a retired cough-medicine salesman with various phrases underlined concerning the true role of women. Then a huge bunch of yellow roses was delivered, which for a time Miss Maidstone suspected might have been sent by Reginald Ritter. During the last week had come postcards, photographs, old newspaper articles about the New Zealand suffragette movement, some cautious proposals of marriage, letters asking for money, and a two-page plea from a poor man who was eighty-four years old and felt Miss Maidstone should let him meet her, to confirm the fact that she was surely the reincarnation of his dead mother. Miss Maidstone replied to each letter in her spidery hand as she sat at the kitchen table day after day, her legs propped up on a cushioned orange-box, the letters and little parcels that kept on being delivered stacked inside a cardboard box she'd lined with pieces of wallpaper. The work kept her busy – she and the rest of the delegation women had been avoiding each other for months, and even when all the hoo-ha had died down after the bus crash, few spoke about the affair in public; it became buried business.

In the evenings Athol sat with Miss Maidstone and read the letters out loud and she never tired of hearing them. She cut out all the best pieces and pasted them into a brand-new scrap-book, on the front of which she'd written 'My Triumph'.

For a few weeks before The Ghoul first appeared there was some excitement when a rich Wellington businessman showed interest in taking over and developing the area of land where Raeleen Cressell's bach had stood, and had plans for turning the area into a Congregational Motor Camp where all denominations could gather at various times of the year to enjoy the peace and harmony of nature. But despite the site being looked over and talked about, nothing came of it, and the town subsided into its problems of facing a slow death, with more folk packing up and departing when no one was looking, and the rest as uneasy as a herd of cows without udders.

When the stifling heat wave appeared to be at its peak and everyone was agreeing with each other that they'd seen the worst of it and that surely some rain must fall any day, the barmaid from the Golden Hope, Miss Marjory Isaacs, was found by one of the late Granny Barker's sons, Sholto, lying strangled to death and sexually interfered with in the old changing shed down on the beach. Sholto Barker had been down there gathering seaweed for his garden. He and his wife Buddleia had been visiting from Tokatoka.

This was several days after more sightings of The Ghoul had been reported. The name for the midnight flasher – now murderer – who had first frightened Mrs Dolly McArthur's sister Mysie out of her wits, sending her fleeing homeward, and had been spotted after dark by a growing number of Sandspit women, including Mrs Gush, had been thought up by Raewyn Scudder's Uncle Frodo who was a hard shot and a wizard at crossword puzzles. Mrs Boona Gush had spotted the spectral sexo one night standing outside the demolished furniture factory and – as she put it – openly playing with himself. She had screamed so loudly that half of Comfort Street was out for hours, brandishing baseball bats and pokers, searching behind every bush and inside every backyard shed without finding a trace of anyone. Most descriptions of him that were made to the Dargaville police by telephone had several things in common: the perpetrator was over six feet tall, he was emaciated to the point of being a skeleton, naked under his coat, and possessed pale features, a strange head and eyes as ugly as a couple of bleached cow-dung pats.

Until Miss Isaacs's untimely and tragic death – for she had been popular in the Golden Hope – the appearances of The Ghoul hadn't been taken all that seriously by many in town. Folk had just been too wound up and worried about their futures, after Miss Maidstone's failed attempts at rejuvenation, along with the unforeseen and escalating drought, days on end without clean water, and a threatened outbreak of a new strain of Asian influenza. There wasn't much else for folk to talk about seriously except what they were to do, how they would survive, should they leave or stay, as most now reckoned the town was surely on its last legs and it was a pound to a pinch of goat-poop that everyone had secretly decided to pack it in and head south, despite dozens having no money for a shift to anywhere except perhaps into the nearest poorhouse.

The death, and the way Miss Isaacs had died, shook the whole town out of its complacent depths. Soon the streets were overrun with speculation and Dargaville police, along with newspaper reporters from Auckland, who published the questionable fact that The Ghoul had already exposed himself to over fifteen Sandspit ladies, was certainly responsible for the horrendous murder of Miss Marjory Isaacs, the popular, young and pretty local barmaid the whole town was in mourning for, and who might be next?

As the weeks went past and more midnight sightings of The Ghoul were reported by parched tongues and local women went in fear for their lives, Miss Maidstone, who appeared to be the only woman in town who hadn't been exposed to the dark terror and had been putting newspaper reports about The Ghoul into a second scrap-book, began to suspect, as she explained later to Athol, who the fiend was. She said nothing to anybody at first but began asking her own cautious questions all over town, after talking Jack Lamb into nailing on new bolts to her front and back doors. Informing Athol that after dark he wasn't to leave her alone inside the house or let anyone in should they knock, she started keeping an old cricket bat beside her bed, never rolling up the window blinds before it was fully daylight outside each morning. Refusing to leave the house unless Athol knew exactly where she was going and by which route, she wasn't scared, she told Athol, she was just taking every precaution she could. Because, despite the police driving over from Dargaville almost every night and roaring up and down the Parade like bodgies in uniform, she was certain The Ghoul was far too clever to be caught or scared off by such obvious tactics.

A lot of folk half believed that The Ghoul was a figment of the local women's imaginations. The growing pressures of unemployment, money problems and the heat were now burgeoning out of control. Those who hadn't yet decided on leaving town were often seen taking furniture or other valuables on trailers off to nearby towns to sell them, or even hanging hand-painted signs outside their front doors advertising possessions, in case visiting sightseers, who'd heard about The Ghoul and had come to lend a hand in the guise of nosiness, might make an offer for a spare bed or a chest of drawers or a set of crockery.

Kezia and Norrie had sent Athol quite a lot of money, which Miss Maidstone had changed into New Zealand pounds by biking down to Dargaville and exchanging it at a local bank. Neither of them let on that they'd become reasonably well off. Miss Maidstone was careful about her spending. What they ate for meals was kept a secret from the neighbours. For, as she said to Athol, it was ten bob to a knob of rancid butter that anyone knowing they had money would be along for a handout. She was as kind as the next bloke, but loans would be as useless as flushing the money down the lavatory. It was every Sandspitter for himself right now.

Along with the money had been a seven-page letter from Kezia telling Athol that she and Norrie were packing up the Gold Coast life and definitely setting off on Randy Delaney's yacht for the Californian coast where gold grew on trees, so they'd been told. Their new mate had fixed it all up. They couldn't sit around waiting for Athol to make up his mind to join them. Australia had been another dead loss and America seemed to offer real answers, it was the centre of everything for the rich, which was what she and Norrie intended to be. Coming back to New Zealand would be just down the gurgler for both of them, back into the bludger's bin – probably living out of the Government's mouldy pocket just as Athol had described Sandspit folk as doing. She and Norrie wanted more out of life than that. When they had got really rich and were living life at the top of the financial heap they'd send him a ticket to fly over. She'd write to him when they landed, she would always love her only son. She and Norrie were both hangdogged he wasn't nicking across to join them.

The letter was covered with kisses and a few lines from Norrie telling Athol that he and Kezia wanted the best for him and for Athol to be a real man and not let being a librarian ruin his life. There was proper man's work out there, he had only to look for it.

Athol didn't answer the letter because Kezia said that they were setting sail in two days' time. He worked out that they might even be in America by the time anything he sent reached Australia. He and Miss Maidstone sat down at the kitchen table one night working out from her *Whitcombe's World Atlas* what route the yacht would take and trying to decide how long the journey might be. After Athol had gone to bed he lay awake in the dark for hours. He thought he might never see Kezia and Norrie again, that this time they were going so far away that anything might happen to them. He felt he should be upset or even that he should cry, but he just lay there staring at the ceiling without feeling much at all, listening to Miss Maidstone snoring in the next room and sometimes calling out 'I'm NOT Madam Muck!' She'd confessed to Athol that she'd been dreaming about Ursula a lot lately. In the night she'd wake up sweating like a baked potato with a vision of Ursula being pursued by a rampant, buck-toothed nun with an uncanny resemblance to Mr Ritter, moving across the opposite wall.

The following morning, the half-naked body of Mrs Enid Mills was discovered by Jack Lamb lying across the bandstand steps. He'd been down there to open up Young's Milk Bar and Grill before the place got hot enough to burn. Mrs Mills had been strangled with a pair of what turned out to be Horace Mills's pyjama trousers twisted into a rope. Horace Mills was found shortly after, minus his pyjama trousers, tied up with rope and gagged with his own underpants, locked into their outside lavatory fifty yards from the open back door of their newly decorated house. The house hadn't been touched – there'd been no burglary, no ransacking – and nothing had been stolen or even damaged, so Horace had little to tell the police when they eventually showed up driving a borrowed truck, as their car had broken down. According to Horace, he'd been fast asleep beside Mrs Mills and the next thing he knew he woke up with something sour-tasting in his mouth and his head covered by a blanket. Then he was being dragged across the lino and out through what must have been the back door. The whole time he heard nothing except a rasping, heavy breathing and a word that sounded a bit like 'sausages' being whispered, but he wasn't too certain, it'd all been done so quickly and no, he hadn't heard anything from Mrs Mills at all, which in hindsight really surprised him.

After Horace had been taken to identify his wife's body and been told that it had been defiled in a particularily nasty way, he collapsed and was driven off to Dargaville Hospital, Miss Maidstone having volunteered to take him in once he was proved medically and emotionally fit to return.

The town closed in on itself after that morning. It was when the double funeral of Mrs Mills and Miss Marjory Isaacs had been carried out, for which Horace Mills had been too ill to attend, that Miss Maidstone announced she was utterly convinced The Ghoul was none other than Mr Ritter himself, changed beyond all recognition. She had suspected as much for a time and couldn't understand why the police hadn't drawn the same conclusions. He was committing the atrocities to get back at her, for refusing to agree to his proposals of marriage, not letting him have his sordid way with her as he'd explicitly asked her to in several letters, and because his mind and sexual needs had gone to and from being deranged for so long that now they had got stuck in the deranged groove and he'd returned with his insanity. He'd also written once to say he might come back so he could take her away to paradise. To a sick mind that could mean into the hereafter. The two hideous murders, and the numerous sightings, were personal warnings, messages, that he was hovering close by and awaiting his moment. It was all obvious to her. When the police got hold of what she'd been spouting all around town they questioned Miss Maidstone for a couple of hours while they sweated and sat red-faced drinking ginger beer on the front veranda of her house. With Athol there to confirm everything she said, Miss Maidstone talked non-stop about every detail of Mr Ritter's past life as she knew it, pointing out that if anyone in town should have been headed down the back alley into the dementia dungeon, then it was Mr Ritter. She'd never been so certain about anything.

The police weren't convinced and after the two hours they thanked her for the ginger beer and the bran biscuits she'd offered and went away. Even Athol could see they'd been unbelieving. Miss Maidstone told him a couple of days later that she knew they'd do nothing. They hadn't listened to one word she'd said. It was up to her to prove the theory and catch mad Mr Ritter herself, with Athol's help. The local police were useless, even if they were now all Dargaville dinkies and supposedly on the ball. They'd achieved nothing yet. They hadn't even spotted The Ghoul as half the township's women had. She was sure if she spotted the wretch she would recognize him as the totally changed and deranged madman Mr Ritter must now be. She knew every crinkled hair on his over-large scalp. Why no one had recognized him by his teeth was anyone's guess, unless he'd lost them after he'd disappeared. There was absolute certainty in her mind that Mr Ritter was The Ghoul. She had no choice but to set out to prove it, come hell or high water.

The first night she went out after dark with Athol, armed with a torch and a couple of meat forks, both of them wearing woollen Balaclavas despite the humidity. A police car stopped them before they'd even reached the corner of Comfort Street. While Mrs Boona Gush kept track of their progress from her front veranda, crouched down behind her potted Daphne bush and holding on to a steel-tipped wooden mallet Miss Maidstone had lent her, one of the two policemen pulling up in the car told Miss Maidstone that if she and Athol didn't return indoors immediately he might arrest both of them. Hadn't they been told there was a curfew, devised by the police because of the recent events? Miss Maidstone tried to argue, to convince them that they needed her expert help, as she knew Mr Ritter more intimately than they ever would. She'd never heard of any curfew. There was talk of slander and a warning to her not to interfere, it was dangerous and hare-brained of her to behave in such a way. She had no proof that Mr Ritter was responsible. In the end Miss Maidstone had no choice but to backtrack to the house, where she spent the rest of the night kneeling behind the railings of her front veranda periodically flashing the torch across the street and crawling on her hands and knees like a soldier in and out through the front door to make cups of tea while Athol was told to watch out the back, to keep the light switched on over the backyard lavatory – it was a perfect place for Mr Ritter to hide.

Hours later Athol fell asleep at the kitchen table. When he did wake up just after dawn he found Miss Maidstone curled up on the veranda steps snoring so loudly that it had aroused some of the Barker clan children. They were lined up on the grass verge in front of the house giggling and staring while eating grapefruit they'd pulled off one of Miss Maidstone's bushes and throwing the peel up on to the veranda in a game to see who could hit Miss Maidstone on the head. Athol chased them away. Miss Maidstone was still asleep when he returned. The batteries in the still switched-on torch she was clutching were long dead. Another night had gone by without incident.

The following night she sat up waiting until the early hours before venturing forth, this time dressed entirely in black, her face and hands camouflaged by burnt cork, carrying a long-handled hammer as well as the torch, a meat fork and a length of rope. She'd let Athol think she would not be going out again after the policeman's warning, but he'd woken up and heard her getting ready. So he pulled on some clothes and followed her at a distance.

The nights at that time were almost as humid as the days, with not a whiff of a breeze even from the sea. As it was nearly a full moon Athol easily kept Miss Maidstone in sight. By the time she left the house the police had stopped patrolling the streets but had parked their repaired car in the Parade, which Miss Maidstone avoided. She legged it across front lawns and through backyards and hid every so often, peering out from behind a bush or over the top of a paling fence, not making a sound, as if she'd been doing night-time surveillance as a professional for years. Athol followed her like a shadow all over town, terrified that at any moment some tall naked fiend might leap out at her. Every shadow made his heart thud. Every small sound drew goose-pimples out on his arms and legs. Yet the streets were quiet and undisturbed beneath the silver-grey moonlight, so deserted that a blind man could have fired a cannon down them and not hit a human soul. After a couple of hours, having been all the way down to the beach without seeing anything except a couple of fighting cats, a dead possum and a hedgehog crossing Anzac Avenue, Miss Maidstone made her way back to Comfort Street still unaware that Athol had been following her every step of the way. As she'd darted from one tree to another and crouched down peering into yards and along side-streets holding the hammer at her side, she'd been muttering in whispers to herself and sometimes let out very loud grunts.

It was three nights later that Athol woke up to hear shouting and a sudden crashing noise. He'd been asleep for hours, having made certain that Miss Maidstone had not crept out of the house again that night before he went off to sleep. She had been making little excursions along Comfort Street like a Home Guard watch – religiously. Pulling on his dressing-gown he raced into the kitchen and through the open back door just in time to see what appeared to be Miss Maidstone dressed in her nightie wrestling violently with someone on the back lawn. She was shouting for Athol at the top of her voice and hitting out with the hammer and by the time Athol reached her side she was squatting on top of the figure, tying its hands together where they'd been twisted behind its back.

Athol helped Miss Maidstone to her feet, trying to calm her down. She was shaking like a tree in an earthquake and told him in a breathless, high-pitched voice that she'd known The Ghoul had been Mr Ritter all along, no one had believed her, she'd prove it now with this tall streak of ugly evidence. But when they rolled the man on the ground on to his back, it wasn't Mr Ritter at all but someone Athol and Miss Maidstone had never seen before, a total stranger, with a squashed nose, black beady eyes and without a hair on his head. Completely bald, he had the most inoffensive face Miss Maidstone later admitted she'd ever seen on a human adult male. He was stark naked under his opened mack and when Athol bent down to cover him up Miss Maidstone suddenly shrieked 'Don't touch the fiend!' and they both leapt back in fright at her voice. The man just lay there staring up at them without moving, with his mouth open. He was bleeding from a knock on the head Miss Maidstone had given him with the hammer and looked either totally dazed or completely demented. He had no resemblance to Mr Ritter, though he did have the same sort of buck-teeth through which his tongue kept darting in and out of his mouth.

Later Miss Maidstone told the police, and Athol, who'd run down to Hinemoa Parade to fetch them, finding them fast asleep inside their car, that she'd been warming some milk on the cooker when she'd looked out the window above the kitchen sink and spotted who she thought was Mr Ritter coming out of her sky-blue painted lavatory, half bent over and wearing a cloth cap, and still wiping himself with yards of her best toilet-paper she kept out there in a bag for unexpected guests. The man's face had been averted before she'd turned to grab the hammer and a length of rope, then crept out through the back door. Somehow in the darkness the intruder didn't see her or hear her approach. She'd leapt on him as soon as he turned his back and was about to enter a copse of bamboo that grew behind the lav. He'd not put up much of a fight. He'd been as weak as a consumptive and just groaned and pushed at her ineffectively with his hands and then started weeping.

The two policemen whom Athol had fetched were only a couple of young blokes of half Miss Maidstone's age. They stared at her with their mouths open after she'd told them what she'd done and had showed them The Ghoul, whom she'd dragged up to sit on the back steps while Athol had been pounding down to the Parade. One of the policemen kept shaking his head and muttering 'Stuff and butter me, I don't believe it', and it was a good ten minutes before either of them could say anything that made any sense. They just kept staring at Miss Maidstone with white faces and bulging eyes as if she was the bravest woman in the country. Miss Maidstone told them without any fuss that they wouldn't have any more trouble from The Ghoul. He was weak because he was obviously ill and half starved, and a while later she helped one of the policemen half carry him out to the car. He was handcuffed to the back seat before the two young blokes radioed through to headquarters. The Ghoul, whose real name turned out to be Selwyn Tuck, simply sat in the car dribbling and grinning to himself, opening his mouth widely and letting his huge, bright pink tongue slip out to lick his chin. He was well away with the fairies, as Miss Maidstone and Athol could see, but as it turned out when details of him were revealed, he had always been a mental case and hunger had nearly finished him off. He'd been on the run for months, all over New Zealand, avoiding capture through police bungling rather than his own ability to survive.

When Miss Maidstone found out that Selwyn Tuck's escape from a high-security mental institution down south had been kept a national secret she raved on for an hour the following day, the head man from the Dargaville headquarters having driven personally all the way on his Puch moped to thank her – it was his day off. By that time she was the heroine of the decade, as far as Sandspit Crossing was concerned. Her photograph again appeared in all the newspapers, this time from Cape Reinga down to Invercargill. Yet the fact that the New Zealand public had been kept in the dark like mushrooms was all Miss Maidstone wanted to ear-wag about even to newspaper reporters – she did not understand why no one had been warned about The Ghoul and she never did get an answer that satisfied her. The only reason for the silence was to avoid a country-wide panic, she was told. Selwyn Tuck had murdered before, decades ago in his youth, and was a helplessly insane sexo who was sometimes quite normal, but he'd been able to roam free without one person except the authorities knowing about it. As far as she was concerned, Miss Maidstone thought it an utter disgrace and ludicrously shameful.

Yet despite her being so riled, outraged and vocal about her feelings, Miss Maidstone was drawn into and delighted at being the toast of the town once more. After the immediate shocks had worn off, folk in Sandspit decided to organize a special Dine and Dance for her at the Masonic Hall, everything to be paid for and provided by the Dargaville police, who were only too willing to oblige, though they were not planning to attend. They were presenting to Miss Maidstone, Mrs Gush being asked to do the honours, a special gift of a wall clock they'd had inscribed as a thank-you from all New Zealand, for her bravery in capturing the demented and murdering Selwyn Tuck, now back in custody with firm promises that until the day of his death he would never again be a free man. There was even talk on the radio of bringing back the death penalty just because of what he'd done, despite his being a lunatic without responsibility for his actions. His mind had completely gone since his capture and was now lost to the world. His whereabouts up until he'd appeared in Sandspit would always remain a mystery. No one else in the North Island had been attacked, according to the police. Selwyn Tuck had managed to get all the way up to Sandspit

Crossing before he'd done rape and murder – the whole business was a real brain-twister.

The Maidstone Mash-Bash, as the planned Dine and Dance got to be called in the few days leading up to it, proved to be one of the most memorable events of Sandspit Crossing's history in more ways than one. The whole town – what was left of it – turned out for the event. It pulled everyone out of the poverty-pit worrying, at least during the hours it was to be held. The Masonic Hall was decorated with so many balloons and streamers and flowers, sent from thankful folk all over the north just for the occasion, that no other event ever held in the ancient hall had equalled it. Everything was organized with such clever secrecy by Mrs Boona Gush, the Dargaville police force and almost every able body in town that Miss Maidstone and Athol had had no idea at all to what lengths townsfolk were going to in her honour. Though she did manage to find out that a celebration had been planned and that she was the reason behind it, because of her brave capture of Selwyn Tuck. Thereafter known everywhere as The Ghoul and voted Devil of the Decade by Women's Institutes and churches all across the country, he was to become the most notorious sexo New Zealand had ever produced.

When Miss Maidstone and Athol arrived at the appointed time outside the Masonic Hall, there was no one standing about waiting to greet them. The doors were locked. At first they thought there'd been a muddle over the exact date. Then after a minute or two the doors were suddenly thrust open from inside and one rousing cheer after another went up into the starlit sky. Miss Maidstone, with Athol on her arm, was ushered in to what long after the event she was to describe as a truly tip-top fairyland. Every inch of the hall was festooned with brightly coloured decorations. Hundreds of green balloons were hanging from the rafters, where giant fern leaves were spread out to resemble a forest ceiling. Huge vases of flowers were lined up along every trestle-table on the perimeter of the floor – polished for the occasion – and a seven-piece orchestra, its musicians wearing dinner suits and gold party hats, were sitting about up on stage below an enormous painted sign which read WELL DONE, OUR GOOD AND FAITHFUL FRIEND, the words of which Mrs Gush admitted to Miss Maidstone were her very own, though there had been quite a panic when the sign turned up with the word FRIEND spelt FIEND and had to be altered.

Just as Miss Maidstone entered the hall the orchestra began to play 'Sweeter as the Day Goes By', which Mrs Gush had chosen, but then the ensemble moved into a waltz and then into a rip-roaring quick-step and the music did not stop once the whole night, as they'd brought in a relief group of melody-makers from Whangarei. Music rocked the walls and blokes were lining up to dance with the honoured guest as if she was royalty, and as Miss Maidstone whispered to Athol during a brief lull, just before the presentation, she was sure glad she'd put on the dog and pulled on her poshest frock and white elbow gloves. Folk had dressed up in their Sunday finest. They hadn't even bothered to do that for Noël Coward on the night of his play.

After the presentation of the inscribed wall clock, which Miss Maidstone wept over and was made speechless by, there was more dancing with songs rendered by New Zealand's most famous radio star, flown up for the occasion – Miss Arlene Macdillacuddy from Christchurch – until plates of food were carried out from the old kitchens behind the stage by all the women who had been on the delegation bus. The food line was headed by the fully recovered Raewyn Scudder who'd come back alone for the occasion and appeared carrying a huge iced fruit cake covered with lighted candles. Miss Maidstone had to cut the cake into dozens of tiny slices with a bread-knife, while Jack Lamb took photographs with his Box Brownie, during which Mrs Gush conducted a rousing chorus of 'For She's a Jolly Good Fellow'.

After that it was more dancing, community singing, games for the children and someone even started a riotous conga line which snaked its way around the tables and up and down the hall and at one stage even into and out of the kitchens. In between there were long speeches from folk who had each once been helped out by Miss Maidstone, those who'd been given jars of her preserves, or been cheered up by and listened to sympathetically as she'd done her rounds around town for years, touching folk's lives. For Miss Maidstone, it was the ultimate accolade of her life. And as she laughed and danced and drank glass after glass of someone else's home-made ginger beer she wept buckets, soaked a dozen handkerchiefs and had her feet trodden on.

It was getting on to two o'clock in the morning with no signs of the party ever ending, when catastrophe struck. Miss Maidstone had made a short speech during which, having become a little tipsy, she'd slipped off the front of the stage but fallen into the arms of Raewyn Scudder's Uncle Frodo from Awanui. Athol had added a few words once Miss Maidstone was lifted back up into the lime-light, and Raewyn Scudder had just come forward and sung a heartfelt but slightly out-of-tune rendition of 'The Victory Side'. She'd announced earlier that she'd found Jesus with her mum in Wellington while they'd been away and was longing to tell the whole world of the boundless joy she and her mum now possessed in their converted hearts, though her dad was still making up his mind. Raewyn had only just finished the last chorus and everyone was giving her the clap while whispering that the hymn wasn't really in good taste considering the flavour of the evening, when a few voices started shouting out from the front of the hall. The doors there and along the sides had been kept shut tight because of a wind that had sprung up outside. At first it was thought that some young blokes were simply acting the goat but the word they shouted spread and filled the whole hall and the word was FIRE!

In a few minutes everyone was charging in a panic towards the doors, as it was generally reckoned that the Masonic must have caught alight somehow, though there was no smoke to be seen. It was soon proved to be far worse than that.

Outside the Masonic Hall the whole of Sandspit Crossing appeared to be ablaze. Flames and sparks and the sound of small explosions filled the night air as if the township had been suddenly transformed into a vision of Baptist hell. For one brief moment, everyone who had fled out on to the Parade was transfixed, like stone statues waiting to be given the breath of life, until women began shrieking and blokes began bellowing for buckets and folk were tearing off in all directions at once. For every building along Hinemoa Parade appeared to have become a blood-red furnace. In the distance more flames were shooting skyward and there were more sounds like explosions until the whole sky was changed to red, smoke billowing out and across the Parade like devil-clouds sent from Beelzebub himself. The wind had grown stronger, drawing the fires upward and across rooftops in an ever-increasing frenzy, and within a very short time it seemed certain that Sandspit was doomed and burning out of all control.

There was no local fire brigade, the nearest was five miles away. Numerous cars and a few trucks were sent speeding off to alert anyone at all who might come to help. Long lines of folk spread out with water-buckets and soaked sacks but their efforts were in vain. The lines broke and were driven back in minutes every time they were formed as the flames spread. Somehow the fires all across town had taken control without one person inside the Masonic Hall noticing a thing, perhaps because all the windows had been covered over with coloured paper and the doors kept shut. The party had become the centre of everyone's world, beer had flowed and the festivities were so involving that anything going on outside had not been noticed.

Athol ran to the corner as soon as he'd seen Miss Maidstone to safety with a lot of other women and children on their way past the Methodist School via Rideout Road towards Kauri Hill, which rose up away from town and out of the immediate danger area. The whole of Comfort Street was like an inferno, every house Athol could see, including his old home and Miss Maidstone's, was blazing, and as he watched, several balls of fire appeared to leap across the street, igniting the remains of the old furniture factory, backtracking on to other houses, towards where he stood, aided by the hot wind which was now spreading the fire so rapidly in all directions that huge sparks were falling down around him and bouncing off the tarmac. Just before he turned and ran, Athol thought he saw a figure standing half-way down Comfort Street holding high what looked like a huge tin-can and dancing, kicking up its legs – but then the figure seemed to notice him and it vanished in an instant, sideways into the billowing smoke. After Athol blinked a few times the figure had gone as if it hadn't been there at all and he'd imagined it.

Athol ran back round the corner, crossing the Parade in the direction of Rideout Road, towards where Miss Maidstone had headed. The whole length of Hinemoa Parade was on fire now, the Majestic Picture Theatre was like a huge funeral pyre, the Masonic Hall already alight across its roof, and as Athol ran there were again sounds like explosions coming from the other end of the Parade and the sparks that were falling caught in his hair, causing him to hit the ground while he beat at his head with both hands and heard himself screeching. Someone helped him up and a blackened face yelled something he couldn't hear, and then whoever it was had gone.

Athol didn't stop running up along Rideout Road through the drifting smoke until he could see ahead of him the rise of Kauri Hill that led up to an area he'd climbed with Norrie and had camped out on for the night years ago. As he reached it he could see what looked like the whole town gathered there on the hillside, staring down past him. Some folk were openly weeping. A few Maori women were kneeling on the grass beating at the ground as they watched homes being destroyed, eaten up by the fire as it spread its fingers through the streets faster than anyone could ever imagine it happening. Athol found Miss Maidstone standing with Mrs Gush, both of them covered with soot and comforting some children. When Miss Maidstone saw him she rushed forward and grabbed hold of him and held him to her, until Athol turned his head and stared down at the worst sight he'd ever seen in his life, the inferno which had once been the town he had never wanted to leave, now a tinder-dry bonfire bigger than any he would ever be likely to see for the rest of his life.

Every person in town had been at Miss Maidstone's celebration at the Masonic Hall, but it was not until nearly dawn that everyone was accounted for. All had headed up the hill except for blokes who were still vainly trying to battle with the blaze. Yet soon even they abandoned their efforts. There were no major casualties, it was believed, except for the town itself, along with everyone's homes and possessions. By the time fire-engines came roaring across from the State Highway there was little left to save, it seemed, and little left to do, for the fires, having taken hold so quickly, were now beginning to die out naturally, the unnatural wind that had forced a rapid, deadly progress of destruction mysteriously fading into a mere breeze. Many hours later, when the sun began to rise up again into a cloudless sky, folk on Kauri Hill looked down with unbelieving eyes on smouldering ruins along every street, from the top of Hinemoa Parade all the way down to the beach track, right across as far as anyone could see to the black shell of the Dairy Board factory and the old cemetery to the north. No one spoke, each stood holding someone else's arm or hand, and as dawn fully appeared, with an already scorching sun, the only sound that could be heard was that of private grief.

Eventually, one by one or in small groups, folk began slowly to descend the hill, holding on to one another, calling out to each other in concern across the heads of others. Miss Maidstone at first would not let go of Athol's arm. They had stood apart from the vast crowd on the hill and had both wept at times, as others had wept. Mrs Gush had moved across to comfort a Maori family who had been all packed up and ready to drive down to relatives in Bradley's Landing that morning, after the big party night, to start up a new life.

Miss Maidstone walked slowly down the hill across the parched grass and around dusty gorse bush, holding Athol close to her side. She wouldn't speak to him or look at him and kept staring straight ahead, her head held high, her face stranger and paler than Athol had ever seen it before, the soot in her hair making her look somehow younger yet older at the same time. As they moved down the last slope on to the tarmac of Rideout Road she stumbled and almost fell. Athol went to grab her, but she pulled away from him then pushed him off with a grunt and kept on walking, heading along Rideout Road towards Comfort Street, alone, her arms held stiffly at her sides.

By mid-morning, the Dargaville police had found a clapped-out rust-bucket of a small van parked in the bush not far from the Bidwell sisters' property, which miraculously had not been burnt to ashes as most houses had been. The van had its doors wide open with the key still in the ignition. It had not been damaged or even singed by the fire either. Piled up in the back were several dozen full kero tins. Even more tins, empty of kerosene, had been discovered all over town, lying on grass verges or abandoned on the tarmac in front of almost every public building and beside almost every house.

That was long after Miss Maidstone had found the grotesque corpse of Mr Reginald Wallace Ritter on the scorched grass verge outside her house. The body was half propped up against her barely damaged whitewashed letter-box. In Mr Ritter's arms were clutched an empty kero tin and several sticks of dynamite, and his grinning, ruined, blackened face with its burnt-out eye-sockets were staring across towards the smouldering remains of what had once been Miss Maidstone's home.

Who Flung the Dung from the Cowshed?

On the night that two young officers from the Dargaville police came to the Bidwell sisters' house to half-accuse Miss Maidstone of having illegally removed Mr Ritter's fire-blackened corpse from where it had been left covered by tarpaulin and surrounded by red tape in front of her undamaged letter-box, there was the worst electrical freak storm ever seen in the whole Northland for twenty years. Mr Ritter's body had vanished. Senior police officers were up in arms about it and had sent men out on a search, despite the ding-dong weather. Hailstones the size of golf balls fell, forked lightning leapt across almost every inch of sky, and the thunder was so loud Mrs Boona Gush spent five hours on her knees under the kitchen table covered by a horse-blanket with a tin bucket on her head yelling above the racket that she believed it was the Second Coming. For half her life she'd cursed Baptists, Methodists, Presbyterians, Plymouth Brethren and Catholics and was now scared stiff she'd end up burning in hell. Miss Maidstone grew so fed up with her going on like a trussed chook she eventually kicked her on the bum with a bare foot and threatened to throw her out of the

137

house. Everyone's nerves were shot to pieces. Sandspit Crossing
had been declared a disaster area, they'd been trampled over by
every authority known to the modern world and the newspaper
reporters had acted like gone-mental emus. Once the same newspaper ninnies heard about the missing corpse, they'd probably
exhibit worse hysteria than Mrs Gush to get the news into the
headlines, Miss Maidstone complained to Athol while she made
billy-tea for the soaked sergeants.

Sandspit Crossing had been evacuated. That is, all except for
Miss Maidstone and Athol. They had refused to leave. Mrs Gush
had nowhere fixed up yet to head off to so all three had moved
temporarily into the empty Bidwell house the morning after the
fire. It was the only place in town that hadn't been burnt to a
cinder. The whole town was cinders and catastrophe, and Miss
Maidstone had also had to cope with verbal diarrhoea from all the
do-gooders and the pesky reporters who'd driven into town in their
bolt-buckets to take over and make her life an even greater misery
than it had been in the first forty-eight hours. At least they were all
gone now. As she told Athol, she was so worn out she could sleep
for a week naked and without blankets on the top of a Maori pa
quite happily if she could be left alone. Folk from out of town had
been as kind as the Salvation Army, but there was a limit to charity.
She was buggered if she'd let herself be taken off to some strange house
miles away where folk would look on her as just another victim. She'd
stop here until she was good and ready to leave and not before. The
papers had been full of the fire, sympathy for the poor victims dripping
like consecrated water from a leaky pipe, but now, after days of
debriefing by the degenerate journos, all Miss Maidstone asked for was
to be left alone to sort things out for herself. She didn't want folk
coming the boiled dog with her, no one had given a stuff for Sandspit
before the fire and the massive fuss-farting had been like some sort of
original guilt from those who reckoned they were some sort of modern-
day missionaries. They had more blankets, food, kitchen items and
clothes than they knew what to do with. Even furniture and someone's
old washing-machine that could be worked by hand had been donated
by well-wishers. All sorts of folk had opened up veins to see that she,
Athol and Mrs Gush were comfortable.

During the days following what the newspapers termed the most tragic inferno New Zealand had ever witnessed (despite that no one except Mr Ritter had been actually burnt to death) supplies and offers of help poured in from all over the country every hour, even after every family in town had been herded off like waifs on the back of trucks, tractors pulling trailers, and in cars, to be delivered to fretting relatives and distressed friends from Dargaville down to Christchurch. The town emptied out so quickly that within days the only folk left wandering the ash-coated streets were Nosy Parkers, police and the reporters who'd turned up by any means they could to stare, gossip, snap photographs and offer advice. No one really understood what had happened, as for a while the police had blocked off certain streets and refused to release the fact that they believed the town's ex-butcher had gone as berserk as a mad bull and then done himself in. It was thought, in due course when that news *was* released to the shocked nation, that Mr Ritter (immediately named and forever to be known as the Kiwi Butcher from Babel) had had numerous accomplices, as it was deemed impossible that he could have accomplished such complete devastation alone. But no trace of anyone else was found, the parked van filled with kero and the dynamite was proved to have been Mr Ritter's and his alone, and the police soon reluctantly admitted publicly that somehow the crazed torcher had achieved everything with his own hands, just as he had died by his own hands in setting fire to himself. They did not release the news that he had left a last letter, addressed to Miss Maidstone, in her undamaged letter-box. In his note Mr Ritter stated that his despair was so great, his heart completely crushed, bruised and badly cracked, that his life had become a hell on earth, and after Miss Magdalen Maidstone's cruel rejection of his proffered soul and pining flesh he'd had no choice but to destroy every particle of the town he and she had known and loved. He held her solely responsible for his drastic actions. This last statement was why the letter was never revealed to the newspapers.

The two sergeants who turned up to stir the pot over the disappeared corpse had faces so ugly that after they'd gone Miss Maidstone told Athol (Mrs Gush being still under the horse-blanket with a bucket on her head though having stopped shouting above the thunder) that the two unfortunates must have both spent years eating peas through tennis-rackets to have achieved their looks. She couldn't imagine any normal males could be that ugly by natural selection. They weren't even religious sorts – she'd asked them. That would have explained something.

She'd been firing off cracks all day, to keep her mind away from the sheer panic and grief she'd had hovering in her tired brain, she confessed to Athol. She didn't want to abandon Sandspit, though she'd no idea why. There was bugger all left to cling on to. For a while, since the fire, it'd been like the end of the world, but she still didn't want to heave to. She had a powerful gut feeling that she wasn't meant to leave for a while yet, and she was more grateful than she could express at Athol's decision to stick with her and for two days she had wept and trembled and Athol had held her hands, wiped her face when she finished and made her blow her nose with a clean hanky. He told her he would always stick by her because she was all he had now, and she responded that they could face the future together and the world could go suck eggs. Sandspit wasn't worth a cracker as it stood at this moment, the weeks ahead if they stayed on might be tough and some days they might even be hungry enough to eat the bottom out of a dead possum if she couldn't come up with some money, but she knew they'd pull through in time. She was a Kiwi and Athol was a Kiwi and they were sturdy sorts, unlike Mrs Gush who'd been born in England and lacked the pioneering spunk all New Zealanders naturally had in their blood. It was part of the package of being born in the snazziest country ever known.

The arrival of the police was the last straw for Miss Maidstone after days of what she reckoned had been gut-churning persecution. Especially as they chose to turn up in the middle of the freak storm with Mrs Gush like an hysterical bush-Baptist and the roof of the neglected Bidwell house deciding to give up and let in half the sky-water in the whole southern hemisphere. Miss Maidstone had placed all the pots and pans and buckets that well-wishers had sent over across every inch of floor. When one of the young men started openly accusing Miss Maidstone of having possibly interfered with the processes of the law by somehow dragging the deceased Reginald Ritter off for goodness knows what reason, Miss Maidstone let fly with every expletive she could think of on the spur of the moment, with a hiss and a roar that sent the two justice-seekers off out the door with embarrassed blushes despite the threat of their possibly being knocked down outside by lightning or drowned by the heaving rain. No one had really suspected her of anything underhand, they said as they left, but they had to do their duty. Miss Maidstone yelled at them, asking why they'd left the body lying there for two days unattended but they both just turned and stared at her with sheepish grins. They didn't come back.

There were no clues as to where the missing corpse could have gone. As far as the police were concerned, they were asking everyone the same questions, but as Miss Maidstone had pointed out (once Mrs Gush had come out from under the table and removed the tin bucket from her head), they were now the only official Sandspitters left in the whole town, so who else were the police asking – the herds of distressed and milk-soured Jersey cows on the neighbouring farms as they lined up outside the sheds? For all she knew, Mr Ritter could have come back to life and walked off to Beulah Land singing the Hallelujah Chorus, she was fed up to her back teeth with what had gone on since the fire. They were having to live for the time being as roughly as pigs in a neglected sty with not much future to look forward to, so why couldn't they be left alone to lick their wounds now all the hoo-ha was dying down. All she wanted was for them to sort themselves out.

Mrs Gush offered the fact that Miss Maidstone *had* been offered alternative homes down-country, she didn't have to stay on and the young policemen were only doing their job, as they'd implied. Miss Maidstone snapped back at her that the police had minds where nobody was home half the time, their scone dough was never properly mixed at the best of times. All they were, were politicians' skivvies, acting as though they had tickets on themselves and knew what they were doing. They didn't know sausages from cowpats. She said nothing about the offers she'd had of a new home. There'd been quite a few but she'd turned them all down.

In the end, long after midnight, she'd got herself into such a state that Athol made her go off to bed. The storm was slowly dying away and first thing in the morning they had to go and fetch buckets of water from the old well near the burnt-out Dairy Board factory. They had no running water in the Bidwell house and no electricity. They were using candles for light and a pump-up primus stove which had been supplied by two sympathetic farmers. Everything had been switched off all across town and service was withdrawn. As the Prime Minister had announced on the radio, the fire-flattened town was empty, everyone had been saved and accounted for. Miss Maidstone, Athol and even poor Mrs Gush weren't even numbers in the book of statistics, Miss Maidstone scoffed. Yet pretty soon they would be left to themselves, she hoped, and even Athol was sure of that, and told Miss Maidstone so as he put her to bed. All down the country there were other major problems for folk to get active and concerned about – there'd been a series of serious earth tremors around Rotorua, Canterbury farmers had gone on strike and had been up to Wellington to chuck dead lamb carcases on to the lawns in front of Parliament House, and the largest outbreak of shingles amongst the South Island elderly ever recorded in the history of Australasia had suddenly erupted into a kind of plague. Athol had been reading all about it in the *New Zealand Herald* – the Sandspit saga was fast becoming just more dead history in the light of everything else. Though several Members of Parliament *were* planning to visit the area in the next couple of weeks once everything had quietened down, to show that the Government did care. It was generally believed and held that the land was to be left to return to its natural state, and in years from now would be sold off as second-class farmland, according to a Government spokesman. No one would wish to live there, after what had happened, it was thought. It'd been a dead-end place anyway with the majority of the populace who'd been talked to, keen to box on regardless elsewhere because there was no possibility of future employment – there hadn't been any since the Dairy Board shut down. It was a case of shape up and ship out, the Prime Minister had announced. Living in New Zealand, as in any new, young country, needed guts and a determination to win by moving on. Athol read excerpts from the man's speech to Miss Maidstone before she fell asleep. Just before she did close her eyelids she muttered that the man had never shown any sympathetic gumption the whole time he'd been in power and wasn't doing so now. He thought he had the goods on everything but he was a simpleton who could have made more impression on the country by renting out his mouth as a car-park.

During the next few weeks, as disaster-hungry sightseers grew less and less and reporters, police and do-gooders went elsewhere to seek immortality, Miss Maidstone, having rescued her miraculously undamaged Harley-Davidson from where she'd always hidden it under tarpaulin behind her sky-blue lavatory which hadn't been too seriously damaged, spent a lot of time biking back and forth between Babylon, fetching supplies, setting them up with a temporary postal service at Kaihu Post Office for diverted mail and generally making certain that they could stay on in the Bidwell house until they knew for certain what was the best thing to do – they might even get turfed out before long. Miss Maidstone told Athol that she'd rather suck all the toes of an unwashed Dutch mud-wrestler than willingly agree to be given a place in a home, which was about all the offered accommodation had amounted to. It'd mean hooray-Henry for her and Athol's life together if that happened. And despite everything she still loved the area dearly, and always would. The air was sweeter here than anywhere else in the world and she just wanted to enjoy a few more lungfuls before the heading-out hour arrived.

The three of them had been along Comfort Street a few times since the disaster had struck. They'd been extra careful, only setting out once the daily influx of the curious and morbid had gone. A lot of the time they hid in the house, as Miss Maidstone wasn't certain of their legal right to be there.

Miss Maidstone rescued the Harley-Davidson, Athol sifted through the ashes where his room had been and Mrs Gush simply stood in the middle of the street with her hands up to her cheeks groaning, refusing to return after the first visit and a grief-filled search through her own rubble – her house along with everyone else's had been destroyed down to the last doorknob and there was little she had left or could find that was worth taking. She still had the posh frock, hat and shoes she'd worn to the Maidstone Mash-Bash, and her handbag into which she had for some reason that night put her savings book and some small valuables and still didn't know why. There was really little left even to look at. The fire, along with the dynamite that Mr Ritter had used to create such great chaos, had rendered such total ruination that everywhere along every street lay ugly piles of blackened rubble and ash. The

Majestic Picture Theatre, the Post Office, the Four Square and even the Golden Hope Hotel were unrecognizable as having been public buildings, as they'd each been constructed on the cheap from wood and spit. Private houses had suffered just as badly and were gone. The Library and General Goods hadn't stood a chance, as they'd been so jerry-built originally and not cared for over decades that, like the rest, their boards and foundations had been a real feast for the flames. Anything of any value that had been left was now gone, hauled away by the owners and, as Miss Maidstone suspected, looters. With the police having set to in search of evidence, the town looked nothing like the thriving settlement it had once been decades ago. Mrs Gush offered to Athol the opinion that Sandspit Crossing must look as bad in its way as parts of London had after the last war. The sight had left all Sandspitters numb from shock and anyone in their right minds who might think they could restore the town would have to pay through the nose to get it all put back right. Miss Maidstone was dead set against any such idea, she'd responded. There could never be another Sandspit Crossing. The place was truly dead and gone and down the toilet for ever more. She was hoping that it would just be left, to become bush again, or maybe farmland one day. She was more than ready to push off herself and start again, when she felt the time was right, she'd never been a member of the Slackarse Club. In two shakes of a dog's hind leg she'd sell her soul to have things back as they had been, but that was just flying in the face of nature.

Mrs Gush confessed to Miss Maidstone and Athol one night as they sat in candlelight playing I Spy with My Little Eye that the reason she'd been reluctant to head off out of it all to start again somewhere was the fact that her stillborn, second daughter, whom she'd not spoken of for years and had always referred to in her mind's ear as Maisy-Day Gush (the Day coming from a great-great-grandmother), was also buried in Sandspit cemetery, along with her husband Endel who'd died of the TB and her daughter Elaine who'd been run over and killed by a tractor. Her whole family was still here and she couldn't understand why other Sandspit folk, who all had blood relatives buried in local soil, could have deserted their dear departed so quickly. It was a crying shame. Yet she knew she couldn't stay on for ever, just as Miss Maidstone wasn't planning to, she liked her comforts too much. There were folk down south, in a place called Elephant Hill near Waimate, who would be more than willing to take her in, they'd been lifelong friends of her late husband and owned a business converting cured sheepskins into tip-top souvenirs. She was too old and tired and troubled daily by her varicose veins to enjoy staying on for very much longer, despite the good company of her dear friends. All her memories of family, photographs and letters and cherished objects had gone up in smoke – she had checked – and there was nothing at all to keep her here except dead bodies mouldering in their graves.

When she'd talked on and on for half an hour without pause for breath, after a tea of corned beef and fried cabbage followed by tinned fruit salad as well as five games of I Spy, Athol was sure Miss Maidstone might try to talk Mrs Gush round, somehow get her to stay just for another week or two, but Miss Maidstone said little, even hugged Mrs Gush and wished her luck, discussing with her how they could get her all the way down to Elephant Hill. Miss Maidstone was all for biking Mrs Gush down on the Harley to Wellington and getting her on board the cross-channel ferry, but Mrs Gush said she'd rather catch a bus from Dargaville and make her own way down south slowly. She hated travelling and couldn't cope with her ailing legs astride Miss Maidstone's big bone-shaker. She had a little money left in her handbag and was sure the Government would help out and hand out if she asked. Others had got quite a lot of financial help. Miss Maidstone could get some if she really wanted, she should give it a pop. But Miss Maidstone just laughed and said that whenever she'd been in the poo in the past she'd always crawled out of it by her own means. She wasn't intending to slip down the toilet-bowl into the sewer yet, she was hanged if she was going to ask for help from the Government, they were nothing more than a pack of dried-up rissoles. No, she told Mrs Gush, she was blowed if she'd let anyone try to shove her off the cliff into charity country.

Miss Maidstone had privately confessed to Athol while Mrs Gush was out the back with the shovel digging a hole to commune with Mother as the Bidwell toilet was busted, that she'd not only rescued the Harley from behind her burnt-out old home, but she'd dug up from the backyard at least half a dozen tins stuffed full of her savings, as well as more money from beneath the floorboards of her sky-blue lavatory – she'd cottoned on to that trick from the wars she'd been through and this was why she and Athol needn't pack it all in now. They were still well off and could go on living in the Bidwell house for a while yet, no worries, she could almost guarantee it, so long as Bathsheba, Dorothy and Maudie Bidwell didn't show up to claim their home back, which seemed highly unlikely. The place wasn't worth even a half-cracker any longer, but they could patch up the roof and fix the smashed windows and live like Lord and Lady Muck – so long as Athol wanted to stay as well. And Athol agreed – there was nowhere else he wanted to go at the moment. He'd sent off a letter to Kezia and Norrie in America and gave the postal service number that Miss Maidstone had organized for a reply, but somehow he didn't really expect much of a response. He was on his own now and over twenty-one, and as Miss Maidstone pointed out, they were a good team, like a couple of healthy shire-horses. They'd be all right. They could sit it out and decide what to do without being rushed.

Every night the three of them listened to the news on the small transistor radio which Mrs Gush had rescued from her outside lavatory in Comfort Street – which, like Miss Maidstone's, had somehow survived the fire but had been knocked on to its side and the bowl smashed to smithereens. As the days went past, less and less was mentioned of the Sandspit torching on the radio. Discussions as to where Mr Ritter's body had disappeared were dropped, as there'd been no new evidence and no trace of it anywhere. There was too much else going on. The outbreak of shingles had turned into an epidemic and had moved north, threatening the whole population of Wellington, and some loony who hadn't yet been caught was setting fire to public buildings all across Auckland.

As Miss Maidstone pointed out, the business over Mr Ritter was almost Raeleen Cressell all over again. The New Zealand Icon had also disappeared totally in a similar way from Sandspit, although Raeleen Cressell's corpse had never actually been spotted and she hadn't been a raving, sex-crazy lunatic. Whoever it had been who'd removed Mr Ritter's corpse, had left behind the empty kero tin and the sticks of dynamite, which inferred they'd been deliberately removed from the dead wretch's arms, and that was a queer thing. She'd give a lot to find out the truth before she waved goodbye. The police were said to be baffled, but Miss Maidstone cracked on that the word bonkers should have been used, which described them much more clearly. During the days they'd tramped all over the flattened town she'd never seen such a display of bungling bozos. When she said that, Mrs Gush spoke up and stated to Athol that Miss Maidstone had always had problems with authority figures. Miss Maidstone just glared at her. Later Miss Maidstone whispered to Athol, after Mrs Gush had taken herself off to sleep on her camp-bed, that she was rather looking forward to when Mrs I-know-it-all Gush decided to head off to Elephant Hill. She could never live for long with another woman, or even another man for that matter. Athol wondered where that left him.

Jack Lamb had left town the day after the fire, cadging a lift down to Kaipara Flats with a Maori family, as he said he'd found out that Beryl was shacked up with Charlie Gregg the suspected Commie in a commune down that way and he had business to settle. He wouldn't be back, he didn't reckon there was much point. The late Mrs Enid Mills's husband Horace was still in hospital and likely to remain there for some time, now there was no home for him in Sandspit to return to, and Raewyn Scudder had fled back to her one-footed mum in Wellington. Mrs Ida Grey had moved to Tolaga Bay, the Barkers had all gone without saying goodbye, Mrs Dolly McArthur and her husband Arthur had left. In fact everyone in town whom Miss Maidstone had known for decades had simply cleared out without so much as a toodle-pip, but somehow, as Miss Maidstone kept confessing to Athol as the days went by, she still felt that everyone was still there, while she was inside the Bidwell house and couldn't see out through the boarded-up windows. It was a bit like what it must feel to have one of your legs off – she'd read about that once. The leg was gone all right when you looked but it felt as though it was still attached to you when you couldn't see it. She didn't want to let the past go. The thought of that hurt like hell.

There was little to do during the day. They passed the time as best they could. Miss Maidstone said they were waiting, but didn't explain what for. Athol privately thought she didn't know and was just delaying everything. Mrs Gush sat about complaining and soaking her feet in a tin bucket of diluted Epsom salts, Athol ended up cooking most of their meals on the primus, and Miss Maidstone had begun climbing up on to the roof and hammering on filched planks to cover up the gaps, causing Mrs Gush to get into paddy after paddy because of the noise and to sulk through breakfast, lunch and tea. It was while she was up there at dusk one afternoon that Miss Maidstone saw what she told Athol afterwards were strange flickering lights moving about, up at the far end of Hinemoa Parade – or what had once been the Parade. She'd seen the lights a few times now but hadn't said anything aloud in case Mrs Gush grew even more involved in her one-woman Frenzy Club. The poor old girl was in a dreadful state as far as her nerves went. They hadn't really settled down since the night of the fire and Miss Maidstone didn't truly understand why Mrs Gush lingered. She would be better off, by the sound of it, heading down south to Elephant Hill and joining her sheepskin souvenir friends.

The lights seemed to hover then dart about just a few feet off the ground and Miss Maidstone suspected they were torchlights, that Sandspit was being regularly visited in secret by persons who might not be up to much good. She'd seen the lights the night after the fire, along near Comfort Street, as well as shadowy figures moving about up there, so while Athol and Mrs Gush were asleep, she'd nicked over to have a reconnoitre but had seen nothing – the lights had gone by the time she reached the remains of the Majestic. She felt in her water, Miss Maidstone told Athol, that something was up, but she was hanged if she knew what. It was rotating her brain crops every night. She was determined to get to the bottom of it. She'd had a thought that it might just have something to do with Mr Ritter, but that was barmy. Whatever it was, it was of human creation. She didn't hold with the crazy modern belief in flying saucers and green bogy men from Mars, talk of which had been on the radio and in the newspapers lately. The sightings were niggling at her, however, made worse by her not having enough to get her teeth into to keep her mind away from imaginings. She was soon to set *that* right, but not in the way Athol imagined.

When Miss Maidstone heard on the radio news one night shortly after that the following day a small delegation from Parliament was to inspect privately – as the announcer put it – what was once the established settlement of Sandstick Crossing, Miss Maidstone almost chucked the transistor set across the room after a few ripe curses and spent the rest of that night pacing up and down the bare floorboards of the kitchen muttering to herself. Long before dawn Athol heard her and saw her, out of half-closed eyes from where he slept on a donated inner-sprung mattress, getting dressed and pulling on a pair of old gumboots she'd found, along with one of the five oilskins they'd been given by a group of Freemasons from Maungatapere. There were such clothes, crockery and all sorts stacked up throughout the empty house. Most of it was unusable. Jack Lamb had shifted the gear into the house before he'd headed off. It had been left on the outskirts of town mostly by the anonymous and no one had wanted it.

Miss Maidstone came back to the house carrying three full flour bags over her shoulders, long after breakfast, during which Mrs Gush had got herself het up and convinced that Miss Maidstone had run off and left them up the boohai without a paddle and was in such hysterical dudgeon when Miss Maidstone did appear that she was packing a sack with all the food she could scrape together, along with clothing, readying herself to walk all the way to Babylon, where she might find a lift south on her trek to Elephant Hill. But Miss Maidstone had other plans. She said she wanted Mrs Gush to give her one last hand before she ran away like a terrified chook.

After she explained what her plan was, Mrs Gush was utterly mortified at the thought of it. It was an hour before Miss Maidstone had nagged and cajoled her into agreeing to be an accomplice. Athol wasn't even asked. Miss Maidstone just assumed that he'd be more than ready to make a stand.

The Parliament delegation was due to show up at any time by then and Miss Maidstone had almost to drag Mrs Gush bodily out into the grey drizzling day with Athol right behind, so they could set themselves up out of sight in the dynamite craters along the Parade wearing the Balaclavas a Women's Institute in Waipapakauri had donated, along with hats and gloves. The clothes were for them to disguise themselves totally, Miss Maidstone said. They should be prepared to run like hell once the deed was done.

Mrs Gush was close to tears as they set out. She'd not been born well over five decades ago only to end up behaving like a wacky revolutionary rebel, she kept trying to tell Athol, but Miss Maidstone was unyielding. They had a duty to make a point, though she had not explained what the point really was, as far as Mrs Gush was concerned.

Athol's opinion that there wasn't much sense to the plan at all if they were to remain anonymous was ignored. Miss Maidstone said she'd staked out the area where she reckoned the delegation would be most likely to stop, and she organized both Mrs Gush and Athol into crouching down to hide behind piles of ashy rubble in the craters when they reached the spot, while she kept watch, having handed them each a bag of what she referred to as political ammo, and both Mrs Gush and Athol were to chuck it with all their might at the buggers once she gave the signal – a low whistle, which she'd been practising with two bent fingers and puckered lips.

They waited in their respective hiding-places for over an hour before anything happened, and got drenched by the drizzle. Miss Maidstone was half expecting the full works – cars of reporters and other hangers-on, and realized that one of them was bound to get caught, but there had to be some sacrifice for protest.

Just after noon a lone shining black car bearing a Government flag slowly appeared from the direction of the State Highway. The car drove with care down towards where they were hiding half-way along the Parade, close to where the Four Square grocery had once stood. As the car approached, Athol could see four figures inside, but he had no idea who they were. A man wearing a cap was driving, but the windows were steamed up and he couldn't see their faces. It was deathly quiet. He could hear a sound that he reckoned was Mrs Gush whimpering. Miss Maidstone had told them that she knew the Prime Minister wasn't going to show up. The radio news had announced that the man was suffering from two badly infected ingrowing toenails and a suspected case of shingles, as the so-called epidemic, having spread north, had had no respect even for politicians. There were numerous public servants falling like flies.

Just after the car had driven slowly past them, its occupants apparently not spotting Miss Maidstone, Athol or Mrs Gush in their well-chosen bolt-holes, it stopped, and the four men clambered out, dressed like pallbearers at a State funeral in black suits and heavy winter coats. As they stood about talking and pointing, Athol heard a low whistle from across the street and immediately reached into his flour sack, closing his eyes and trying not to breathe in the foul smell. Holding his breath, telling himself that this was the looniest thing he'd ever done, he took out a handful of Miss Maidstone's ammo and scrambled to his feet, opened his eyes wide, aimed as well as he could, and threw.

The news was on the radio by tea-time. All through it Miss Maidstone whooped and laughed and kept shouting 'Eureka!' and clapped her hands in glee while Mrs Gush sat on floor cushions with her own well-scrubbed hands hiding her face, still whimpering and complaining that if anyone ever found out she'd been involved in the crazy plan she would immediately die of embarrassment, but all three of them would probably end up in gaol anyway and the key thrown away. She'd sworn to Miss Maidstone that she had thrown her own ammo as best as she'd been able to and it wasn't her fault that her aim had been too high and that most of it had gone across the top of the car and landed near Miss Maidstone's hiding-place. One piece of ammo had fallen on Miss Maidstone's head and nearly knocked her out.

According to the news, the upstanding Members of Parliament, with a chauffeur, who had, in their own free time and with grave concern, decided to visit the destroyed northern settlement which had featured so much in the news during past weeks, had, on arrival, been pelted with so much cow-dung by a person or persons unknown that they were each being treated in a Whangarei hospital for shock and suspected infection from the befouling. They were appalled at the thought that any good, law-abiding New Zealander might have been involved, and had resorted to such an infantile and totally meaningless gesture. The attack had been so swift and unexpected that it'd been only moments before each of the Honourable Members were covered head to foot with cow excrement, most of it so fresh that it had created extreme distress and some of it so hard that bruising and several sprained fingers had been caused. The delegation had been able to get back into the car only with help from the chauffeur, who was to receive a befitting mention in the next Sessions. No one had been seen to do the deed, the day had been dull and foggy, but the chauffeur had very quickly driven the Honourable Members away from the scene with remarkable speed, fearing that the attack might escalate into some more serious incident, had he delayed. With hindsight he was certain that he'd half seen out of the corner of his eyes a dangerous-looking figure in a mask, brandishing a gun, and the Members, afterwards, had begun to believe it had possibly been some sort of Communist-based, deliberately planned plot, yet no one had since come forward to claim responsibility.

The item dominated the news for twenty minutes, experts having been brought into the studio to discuss the whole affair, and it was added that the Prime Minister, if well enough, was to be asked for a statement before the day was out. The whole area had been searched but no one had been discovered lurking about. The attackers were understood to have escaped so quickly that they could only have been professionals, it was thought.

Miss Maidstone sat riveted (occasionally yelling out 'Liars, liars!') as words like juvenile, futile, unproductive and preposterous were bandied about over the air-waves but somehow in the end she acted disappointed, when blame was directed at left-wing radicals or Reds who were bound to be hiding under a lot of New Zealand beds and must be found and hauled out and dispersed, because the country DID NOT NEED such behaviour, when crisis after crisis was being skilfully handled by the country's hard-pressed leaders. No one suggested the possibility that anyone could be still living in the wrecked town, and the attack might have come from that quarter. The whole affair was kept within the political paddock – an attempted act of terror was the general consensus, simply to stir up resentment on all sides of the House while the country was still in chaos.

When the news turned to the shingles epidemic and about a woman from Epuni in Lower Hutt who had been found harbouring the long-dead corpse of her twin brother in her bath whom she'd hated and killed by administering poison, Miss Maidstone switched the radio off and stomped off out the back. An hour later Athol found her still sitting out there on an old tree-stump staring across towards the beach. She confessed that she'd impulsively collected the dung that morning from a local farm cowshed when no one was around and the throwing of it had probably been a waste of effort and childish, it hadn't achieved anything, but it had certainly cheered her up at the time and made her feel she was getting her own back at life in general. The future for her and Athol, every-thing she had held dear to her heart, still seemed bleak and right up the stagnant creek. She was only a speck of fly dirt on the map, she said. What could she do to change anything, to rebuild or be listened to? She was just a frustrated old chook with spud mash for brains. But then she grinned and looked up into Athol's eyes and reckoned that while she'd been chucking the dung and while they'd been running like hunted stags back towards Anzac Avenue she had felt like a million dollars and chockful of real Kiwi spunk.

Mrs Boona Gush left two days later. She'd had enough of the gumbooting gypsy life, she told Athol. Her body couldn't take it. She felt like a criminal, having flung the dung. She packed a haversack with food and some of the clothes which had been given in charity, said her goodbyes and was gone in an hour, Miss Maidstone badgering her into accepting a lift on the back of the Harley-Davidson at least as far as Babylon, or further if she found she was able to cope with her legs on the back of the bike after all. Miss Maidstone had wept as Mrs Gush said goodbye. She'd known Boona for so many decades, Miss Maidstone said, and felt like she was losing a blood-sister, the last of the true Sandspitters. Mrs Gush wept for a while too, but Athol could see by the look in her eyes that she couldn't wait to get away. She was terrified the authorities were about to show up, had been going on about that all through breakfast every morning and during the night, peering through the front door across the deserted town as if she fully expected the Army to appear, with tanks and burly men with rifles. Athol kept telling her he didn't reckon that anything more would happen, politicians were used to dung-chucking, but Mrs Gush wasn't con-vinced. She'd never heard of anyone in all her lifetime throwing cowpats at Parliament Members before, it'd been a shameful thing to do.

Athol watched them from the front yard as Miss Maidstone manoeuvred the old machine down along the Parade, Mrs Gush hanging on for dear life and letting out little cries as they veered in and out of blackened timber and twisted corrugated iron and pot-holes. When they had moved out of sight, he sat down on the broken steps of the house and thought about Kezia and Norrie. There'd been a letter from them at the post service box when Miss Maidstone had been there to check the day before. The letter was nine pages long and in it Kezia wrote that she and Norrie had really landed on their bums in American butter after a lot of slippery struggle. They were living in Hollywood, California, and were renting an old mansion that long ago had belonged to a silent film star. She couldn't remember the star's name but she had been a famous one, according to Randy Delaney, and she'd let Athol know who it was in her next. She and Norrie had been almost knocked off their perches by his crook news, what a terrible wallop, she couldn't believe Mr Ritter was responsible, she'd always found him to be the perfect gent and a real man, unlike most New Zealand males. Didn't Athol want to get over to them now, she'd send the fare or she might be able to get him a ticket and she'd be sending him some money anyway very soon. They were rolling in loot (one night she and Norrie and Randy Delaney had filled the bath with dollars and sat in it without a stitch on, drinking champagne) – Athol would be a hot-headed nincompoop not to take up the offer to join them, after what he'd been through. Randy Delaney was really keen for Athol to come across, he had a soft spot for young men.

According to Kezia, Norrie was raking in thousands of dollars every week. She even had a part-time Puerto Rican maid and they were thinking about a butler – there was an agency in Los Angeles that supplied real English butlers with diplomas in home care. Of course Norrie had to carry a small gun and have a bodyguard with him whenever he went out, Randy insisted on it, but theirs was sure a beaut life and New Zealand was a dead loss in comparison.

Athol sat and thought about the letter, grinning to himself, staring across at the mounds of rubble, the collapsed and broken power-poles and the huge holes in the ground where Mr Ritter had let off his dynamite, wondering how Miss Maidstone might fit into such a life. There was hardly a sound anywhere nearby, except for the sea behind him. The sky was the deepest shade of blue he could ever remember seeing. He felt he was the last person on earth and he sat there without moving for hours, not having decided anything at all about what he should do or where he and Miss Maidstone could go. And when she did finally come roaring back across the blackened earth honking the Harley's horn and shouting out, he was never more pleased to see anyone. After she'd clambered off the bike and yanked off her goggles they hugged each other for a long time and both got so choked up they started to laugh.

A few days later, just as dark was forming around them, and they were sitting out at the front of the house staring up at the millions of stars forming in the perfectly clear sky, after a tea of fried lamb chops and mushrooms followed by some apples Miss Maidstone had also brought back from the farm, a figure appeared in the far distance, walking slowly towards them along the centre of the Parade. In the ghostly half-light the figure's strange clothing seemed to shimmer. Miss Maidstone got to her feet, pulling Athol up with her, peering forward into the gloom, her mouth dropping open. When the figure saw them he slowed down to a shuffle, spread out his arms and smiled. He was wearing a long white robe which hung to the ground and was gathered in at the waist, had sandals on his bare feet, his long hair whiter than snow and a beard to match. For a moment Miss Maidstone didn't say anything but she gripped Athol's arm in hers. She had just been telling him that she reckoned it was time for them to leave now, she could feel it in her water, they could head south together on the Harley and face whatever they'd have chucked at them when it happened. Then she told him about how she had once wickedly coerced her sister Ursula into squirting two of the nuns who'd taught them at Convent School in Dargaville with an ink-filled water-pistol from the front yard of their aunt's house as the nuns were passing by. Ursula had hated her for years because of that. They'd both been whipped with leather straps the following day by the Mother Superior and had had to write out five hundred Hail Marys. So long as she stayed on in the area, she confessed to Athol, the past would hold on to her heart like a vice. She wanted to get as far away from Northland as they could – there'd be new adventures somewhere down-country, in other places, she was certain of it.

After they had carried on staring at the approaching figure, who was steadily moving closer towards them, his arms still out-stretched, his face grinning like the Chesire cat, Miss Maidstone let out a whoop and stepped forward, as she said she could see the man clearly now. To Athol, in the fading light, the man looked like an apparition, but then Miss Maidstone started to laugh and said to slap her across the lips with a pound of boiled tripe – if she wasn't mistaken, they were about to shake hands with Jesus Christ himself.

A Prophet, an Abduction and a Busload of Grinning Lips . . .

During the few weeks when so many outbreaks of shingles were reported up and down the country that the Government was forced to announce vast areas to be no-go disaster zones, earthquakes were registering up to the rafters on the Richter scale and had been knocking down buildings, cracking the earth and pummelling the population of certain towns and cities from Hamilton to Invercargill. So far, none had occurred in Northland.

At the same time, the Reverend Fulk – for it was he who had turned up in a robe and whom Miss Maidstone had jokingly identified as Jesus Christ – began knocking up a modern Bethlehem temple in the middle of the cleared Hinemoa Parade, with the help of a small fortune, a vision and three partners who had always been, so the Reverend had informed Miss Maidstone and Athol, his faithful followers for decades and destined to assist him in banishing corruption and sin for all eternity and offering everlasting life.

Miss Maidstone hadn't believed a word the Reverend Fulk had said that day when he'd showed up, let alone understood any of it. His vision was straight out of a *Crazy Comics Annual*, she reckoned, despite fervour dripping from the man's tongue like melted lard. Yet the Reverend had also acted so creepy and had grovelled so strangely, she confided in Athol that she'd been sorely tempted at first to ask him if he'd been turned into a goblin, or how much he'd charge to haunt a ten-room house, but she'd kept her chops shut and her flippancy at bay out of a kind of dazed politeness. She didn't even realize who the character was for a while, because of his queer outfit and Santa Claus beard, though she knew she'd seen him before, a long time ago. She had learnt a long time ago to expect anything in Sandspit Crossing. It was when he explained, as if she should remember, that he wasn't the Reverend Fulk of Gospel Crusade fame any longer but wished to be known (just for the time being, he insisted) simply as Mr Enoch Elisha Fulk, that her mind had trundled back all those years to when the ugly shyster had first come to Sandspit to save souls but had instead created chaos and a certain amount of grief as well as causing bones to be broken. When she remembered that, she told Athol, she felt a little brain-smacked and knew she couldn't afford to trust anything he said at all, even if he was putting on the posh dog and was all dressed up like a Messiah. In fact she wouldn't have minded giving him a hard kick where his mum had never kissed him for what he'd stirred up in the past, but with the gift of the gab and his dazzlingly white teeth he'd managed temporarily to baffle her with bull-poop so that her instincts and clear thought had disappeared upstream with the trout.

It wasn't just a matter of a bad penny turning up again, there was something not at all right in the ozone surrounding his face-ache smile. He stood there outside the Bidwell house in his robe and dusty sandals and told them in cocoa tones that he'd been successfully touring Australia as the Reverend Fulk with his Gospel Crusade of Hope when one day near Alice Springs he'd been struck on the head by a freak flash of lightning and was given a blinding vision about the future, which had changed his outlook as well as his appearance. On his return to New Zealand, and hearing about the Sandspit Crossing tragedy, the town where he had saved record numbers of souls from damnation and had faced the real Satan in person, he had finally realized where his true mission in life lay. To build a Bethlehem temple on this troubled slice of New Zealand soil, with money he'd accrued from preaching, along with a fortune

he'd accidentally won in a new State lottery in Victoria. Building
the temple here was to be the beginning of the final triumph of his
soul-gathering life. He'd even given up saving souls as a mere
preacher in the meantime to do so. For what he had in mind – what
he had been made to realize about himself from his Australian
vision – was to take all of New Zealand and the rest of the world
back to biblical times, as well as updating religious history. Time
would prove that he could do it. He had been scouting around the
area secretly with his partners for some weeks now, while camped
out in the bush, getting minds in gear for his divine plans.

That last piece of information solved the mystery of the shining
torchlights, as Miss Maidstone admitted to Athol after the man had
finally stopped gas-bagging and was gone. It must have been Fulk
and his partners she'd spotted up near Comfort Street, on much
more than one occasion.

He had a caravan now, Enoch Fulk told Miss Maidstone and
Athol, in which he lived and meditated and mingled with mystic
truth. It was pulled by a Fergusson tractor painted black. The
caravan was all-white, inside and out, and the two man-made
objects represented earthly good and evil – evil pulling the good but
with the good never far behind. The white caravan would outlast
the tractor, as tractors had a tendency to break down or wear out,
especially the make he'd chosen, that was about the strength of it.
He was going to use that symbolism when he gave his sermons on
Kauri Hill, but as yet he hadn't revealed his true identity to the
world at large and was still gearing up. He would reveal all, once
the Bethlehem temple was knocked together. He wouldn't mind
Miss Maidstone having a part, and joining his world-changing
divinity, if she was interested. He'd heard a great deal about her
from all sorts up and down the country.

Miss Maidstone and Athol found it about as easy to take in what
Mr Fulk flapped his gums about for over half an hour as shoving a
pound of butter up your bottom with a knitting-needle on a hot day.
As Miss Maidstone said after he had left on that first appearance,
though he'd flogged his chops at her for over thirty minutes, she'd still
not understood a damn thing, never mind his assurance that the
reason behind his plan would eventually be made clear, not just to her

but to the whole world. She had only to find faith and patience in her heart. She'd count herself a lucky woman being right on the spot where it was all about to happen, she should just wait and see.

Miss Maidstone reckoned that Fulk was far more gone in the head than just well off his trolley. His plan was utterly loony. He had quite simply, in her personal book of memory, been a bull artist from way, way back, but now she could add insanity to the list. How could he expect to convince anyone that his sincerity – a word he kept spitting out – was genuine, after all the strife he'd caused all those years ago? He must know that she remembered what he'd once helped to cause, he'd probably conned hundreds of simple folk. No one could put a cow-cover over a horse and expect to get milk from it in the morning, she told Athol. The whole business of his showing up was sheer kibosh and a great disappointment, and if what he'd inferred about his true identity had some truth and that this was Sandspit's aftermath – getting visited from a gone-crazy coot like Fulk as well as from no-hoper politicians – then it was just as well she and Athol *were* thinking of moving out. Sandspit Crossing was history, and they may as well face up to it. Yet she was busting with curiosity to see what Fulk had up his sleeve. Her mind was going haywire with all sorts of possibilities. Perhaps he'd even perform a few miracles.

Enoch Fulk had parked his black tractor and all-white caravan at the far end of town just beyond the remains of Comfort Street. After that first visit he didn't come back across to the Bidwell house again. Miss Maidstone and Athol kept as close a watch on his movements as they could from a distance, but it seemed that his plan to build the temple was genuine. The day after his appearance they spotted him driving a truck, laden with planks of wood, corrugated iron, bags of nails, paint and all sorts, and pulling behind it a small bulldozer on wheels. After a while his three partners also showed up and were all over the place, lugging debris off Hinemoa Parade, measuring, hammering and generally looking as if they knew what they were doing. Miss Maidstone was intrigued. The three partners looked even more queer than Fulk and had the widest hips she'd ever seen on any males. A large marquee was even erected overnight in which Fulk's partners appeared to be sleeping and from where, after dark, Miss Maidstone could swear came the sounds of strange high-pitched singing voices and a sort of chanting. She was longing to nick over there for a reconnoitre but felt too inadequate. Fulk gave her a touch of the heebie-jeebies. His eyes had been as crazed as those of a sex-starved bull.

It was when Athol came back the next morning from having a quiet look around and told her who Enoch Elisha Fulk's helping hands were that got Miss Maidstone hunting for the old telescope she'd discovered at the back of an empty cupboard just after they'd shifted into the house. Athol said he hadn't recognized them at first but Fulk's partners were none other than Maudie, Dorothy and Bathsheba Bidwell, and each of them had had their hair cropped shorter than a man's, their faces were nightmares and as tanned as tired leather, they wore stained overalls and gumboots and acted as if they hadn't known who he was when he'd called out to them across the blackened remains of the Four Square grocery. Miss Maidstone was totally stumped over that piece of news. She couldn't figure out why the sisters hadn't come straight across to the house – it was still their house, as far as she knew, and they'd been her good mates way back before they'd disappeared off the face of the world. She didn't know what to make of any of it, nor what was the best thing to do – get across there smartly and greet them, invite them back for a cup of billy-tea, or just stay put and await developments. Athol told her that the sisters had acted really peculiar, he could have sworn they'd recognized him, but they had just stared across at him with vacant eyes like cows chewing cud. They hadn't made any move to be friendly and looked as rough as guts and touched in the head. He couldn't have changed all that much in seven years, he was sure they knew who he was. In the end Miss Maidstone did nothing except keep constant watch from the front steps with the telescope, focusing on each sister and admitting to Athol that they had indeed changed almost beyond recognition, as if they'd been rescued from years indoors at a white-slave market.

Enoch Fulk and the Bidwell sisters were as busy as bees with bums full of honey during the next couple of weeks. They made no effort to come across to the house, and Miss Maidstone made none to encounter them when she headed off on the Harley-Davidson for supplies, taking the back route, down along past the beach behind the old Dairy Board factory remains. She said nothing to anyone in Babylon about Fulk. He and the sisters, having cleared all the rubble from along Hinemoa Parade, then began work on the temple – which Miss Maidstone said looked nothing like any temple she'd seen in all the history books she'd read. It took shape very quickly as all four were out working on it from dawn until dusk and after dark, with hammers and saws, white paint and torches, appearing to live on bread and scrape and working so fast and shoddily that Miss Maidstone began to have a suspicion that Fulk was moonlighting, that he'd not had any go-ahead from the authorities to build on the land and might just be getting the place knocked up as quickly as he could, after which he could claim some legal rights, as the building was intended for religious purposes, if anything at all about this ding-dong event was to be believed. True, Fulk might be a loony but he wasn't stupid, or he hadn't been in the past, and she'd bet a few shillings that he hadn't changed. Once a shyster always a shyster, she told Athol. She and Athol spent hours every evening sitting in candlelight discussing what Fulk might really be up to, if all he'd told her was lies – it was beyond both of them as to why he and the Bidwells had suddenly turned up out of nowhere, why the sisters were acting so strangely, and where Fulk might have been for all those years. Why build a temple way out here of all places, Miss Maidstone kept asking, who would come to visit, except the odd escaped cow or a couple of the wild pigs which were starting to roam the whole area now that nature was taking over? She didn't think there was any reason to lay eggs and strat a fuss, even though she reckoned Fulk didn't have any rights at all to do what he was doing, but she was getting to feel as uneasy as a voiceless hyena about it and her brain juices were bubbling.

One morning, chocka with curiosity and not prepared to sit about any longer, she pulled on her gumboots and set out to where she could see Fulk and the Bidwell sisters gathered at the side of the temple, which was now almost completed and being painted. They'd even constructed a huge wooden cross, and as Miss Maidstone headed their way, appeared to be considering how they were going to raise it up on to the roof, as Fulk had ropes and a pulley and kept pointing upward, though the sisters were staring off in a different direction with wide-open mouths. Miss Maidstone had never seen a building, even a garden shed, being constructed so quickly or with such lack of plan before. Insanity dripped from the whole shebang.

When she reached them, Enoch Fulk was all smiles and forelock-touching, but Bathsheba and Maudie stared at Miss Maidstone as if they were scared stiff of her or thought they'd seen a ghost and Dorothy went redder than a tree tomato, turned her back and started shaking all over in a kind of fit. They hurried away, linking arms, after Miss Maidstone had reached to within a few feet and then Fulk took over, blocking her from getting too close to the sisters after saying something to them in a low, threatening voice. He said he had wanted to have a word with Miss Maidstone, though they'd been far too busy, but when Miss Maidstone asked him what was wrong with the Bidwells as they looked ill, he became as tight as a gnat's bottom on that subject. To Miss Maidstone the sisters looked at death's door. They'd each lost a great deal of weight and acted as jittery as hens in front of a starving fox. Enoch Fulk, in his strange way of talking (she told Athol afterwards that she was sure Fulk had sometime in the past suffered a stroke or had had a bad bout of angina), told her that she must find patience and trust, the sisters had experienced some extremely difficult times since they'd fled from Sandspit Crossing all those years ago where the Devil had exposed himself to them, affecting their behaviour and bruising their souls – that, like the man who hatched, patched, matched and dispatched, he, Enoch Elisha Fulk, was here to cure and heal the sick and the ailing too but he was out to heal the souls of men and women, not just the ageing, decaying body as doctors did. He talked so much to Miss Maidstone without telling her anything she truly wanted to hear that she reckoned to Athol the wind had been blowing up the skirt of his now filthy robe and waggling his tongue and that all he'd said was sheer rot.

The Bethlehem temple, as Enoch Fulk had insisted to her that his rickety construction be called, looked less like a place of religious shelter than a shark-bait shed. A good gust of wind would flatten it to the ground if a storm brewed up. It was all odd angles and out of proportion like a short-sighted farmer's hen-house, though it had real windows of artificial stained glass made from plastic. There was an open doorway leading inside through a double door which had yet to be screwed on and was an irregular shape. The roof was sloped with the highest point at the back and there were no foundations, and on top, where the wooden cross was probably to be placed, stood an unpainted billboard. Boxes of candles were stacked up in the doorway with an oval-shaped container like a misshapen coffin with a glass lid. Enoch Fulk explained that the building was, in the long term, just a temporary temple, and not to let it put Miss Maidstone off or worry her. Once he had announced himself to New Zealand, said who he really was and why he had chosen this evil place to return to, folk all over the country and overseas would be begging to provide him with buckets of funds to build a real Heavenly Haven, and, he hoped, enough donations to rebuild the entire town as the New New Zealand Bethlehem. What he said after that, as Miss Maidstone reported to Athol later that day, was what she hadn't wanted to hear despite its exciting her: she enjoyed a chunk of spurious confession even if it came from the insane. For when she asked Fulk what on earth he was going on about, she still didn't understand, he smiled with all his teeth and told her quite matter of factly and calmly that he had been reborn as the New Jehovah, that Sandspit Crossing, he knew now, had been the pit where the earthly form of the Devil had been lurking for years, but the Devil was now vanquished – burnt up in the flames of his own hell. Fulk had evidence, he said, right over there in his all-white caravan, of who the Devil had been. Satan had lived right here in Sandspit Crossing. He, the New Jehovah, was to offer all New Zealanders divine, eternal life now that the Devil was dead, and he was telling Miss Maidstone of this great revelation because he was set on having her beside him as his right-hand man.

Miss Maidstone told Athol that when Fulk had talked about the Devil, she'd known for sure, however crazy it seemed, that he was somehow referring to poor Mr Ritter, but he'd simply refused to elaborate. And never mind her becoming Fulk's right-hand man and joining this Geeks Glee Club – with her Christian name Magdalen she was really surprised he hadn't asked her to be his mother. Or perhaps he was hoping to get together some sort of geriatric harem, for the whole scheme was about as far away from sanity or religion as an Italian-speaking donkey would be from giving virgin birth. How he'd been able to stand there and tell her that he was the New Jehovah without blushing from sheer shame at the sacrilege or even laughing about it was more than enough to convince her that his brain had been truly gassed somewhere along the line or been replaced. Why on earth the Bidwell sisters had got caught up with him again was beyond comprehension, unless he'd hypnotized them or had them totally under his power in some other way. They looked as if they might even be on drugs. She would laugh for a week if she didn't find it all so preposterous and scare-mongering. What a truly crummy end to Sandspit Crossing, to have this lunatic of an oxygen-gobbler thrust on them just as they'd decided to call it a day and head off into a new life. What the heck was she to do about this one? It was queerer than the Raeleen Cressell affair, or Selwyn Tuck The Grisly Ghoul.

That night in the Bidwell house she came up with an idea that the only way to prevent Enoch Fulk from making a complete fool of himself and finishing Sandspit Crossing's final days as a real sick joke was to destroy the so-called temple before the whole affair got out of hand and he started spreading his news. She and Athol could go off and try to get some help, but the nearest place was Babylon, where folk wouldn't know what to do, they wouldn't know poop from dried dates until they'd been chewing for a week. She and Athol would just have to sort this out by themselves. She didn't want to leave until she knew Sandspit could be left to return to bush and weeds with dignity. It was sticking up her gunga to think that Enoch Fulk would make the place into a national laughing spot. Tourists would come from all over if the news got out. They'd split their sides laughing.

While the building of the temple had been going on day after day, the whole length of New Zealand from Auckland down to Stewart Island in the far south appeared to be certainly in the tight clutches of the worst crisis since the last war. It was believed that folk were actually dying from the virulent strain of shingles gripping the country, and the earthquakes were causing more havoc than if the World War II had actually taken place on New Zealand soil. The Government was split in two by pressure, indecision, argument and illness – politicians and public servants were collapsing daily, it seemed, from shingles and stress and were being rushed off to hospital. To top it all, there were outbreaks of thieving on a massive scale, looting was becoming as frequent as Baptist prayer meetings and arson was turning the skies red and the cities into cesspits. Almost the entire country, or huge pockets of it, except for the winterless north, it was reported on the news via Mrs Gush's transistor radio which she'd left behind, was rapidly heading into a haven for the damned and not one person knew why. Overseas, in Australia and America and even in the United Kingdom, life went on as normal while New Zealand was rocked by the earth tremors and seething with a savagery on all sides as if human minds had been poisoned. Miss Maidstone couldn't help but wonder if it was all connected in some way to the lunatic in his white caravan, but the thought was just too goofy.

The morning following Miss Maidstone's decision to try to put a stop to Fulk's fanatical fiddling she opened the front door of the house and there, not five hundred yards away across the flattened land, stood the finished, white-painted shack in all its jerry-built glory, with its corrugated-iron roof and the huge wooden cross in place on top, which Enoch Fulk was apparently intending to use as his Bethlehem headquarters. As Miss Maidstone confessed to Athol over a breakfast of fried bread, tinned mushrooms and fresh milk from a billy she'd fetched from a nearby farm, it was enough to addle anyone's brain completely. They should have headed off out of it earlier but she had to see this through. No one in the immediate district had appeared, to see what was going on – the fear of shingles pressing north from Auckland and the worry that earthquakes might start up locally had caused folk to slam their doors and pull down their blinds, Miss Maidstone reckoned. They were on their own but she was blowed if she'd let a crazy preacher turn the remains of the town she'd loved into a travesty – if the newspapers got hold of what Fulk was trying to do they'd be so far upstream with hysteria they'd leave the trout dead. The thought of what Fulk's vision might lead to was starting to give her dry horrors. The Bidwell sisters were acting like the living dead, they walked about looking like a trio of prunes with complexions similar to oxidized potatoes and just stared at her. That had scared her more than anything, she told Athol. She knew somehow that Fulk had a dangerous hold over them. It was time for action. She'd got her thinking-cap well and truly pulled on her head and her energy at the ready. Athol told her he was very much relieved – she'd been repeating herself and yacking away for days about it and driving him up the wall, and if Miss Maidstone did intend to do something, then let it be soon.

Athol had had another letter from Kezia. She told him that she was not only still keen but insistent that he came to join them in America. She would wait for his reply as soon as he got her letter – she knew how long her letter would take to reach him. She and Norrie had an English butler now. He was called Hamish, but unfortunately he had a bad harelip. Norrie was having a heart-shaped swimming-pool built in their backyard, and the silent film star who had once owned their mansion had been called Panola Poli and had made over thirty films before sound came along and ruined her career, as she had a rotten speaking voice. Kezia was trying to find out more about her, she said, but local folk were proving to be a dead loss about the past and no one acted all that interested. Norrie reckoned that Kezia could write a beaut book about Panola Poli and make a mint and Athol could help her when he got there. If only they could get all the jazz together – a best-seller dripped from what they already knew. Randy Delaney had connections for getting a book published. He was over the moon and skiting to all his bodyguards that Athol was probably going to join them.

She would donate her right arm for medical research to have Athol in Hollywood right now, she wrote. There were beautifully bonzer blonde girls on every street-corner just waiting for the right young man to come along and pick them up. Before long Norrie reckoned that he and Kezia could well end up becoming half-millionaires. There they were, being served breakfast in their pink four-poster bed every morning, basking amongst the famous all day and meeting future film stars at parties while their only begotten son was out in New Zealand living in a burnt-out town with a spinster while around him the whole country appeared to be sliding down the toity. She and Norrie had been following all the queer news and were going mental about the shingles epidemic, the earthquakes and the looting. It was enough to develop a dozen goitres – both of them were so adamant about getting Athol away from all that strife that they were fully prepared for Miss Maidstone to be brought over with him, as Athol seemed so worried about her. It was a fine thing his wanting to take care of an old chook like her, but it was a bit on the nose, her expecting Athol to stay with her out there in the circumstances. He was being a real Uncle Willy – where the heck had he been when they had handed out the brains? His brains surely couldn't have come from her and Norrie. Folk out there might well think that Kezia Buck had been the sort to have swum after the troopships – she knew she'd done wrong when they'd upped and left him but she had a real beaut life waiting for him now in Hollywood. She loved him with all her heart, and Miss Maidstone would be more than welcome to join them. They had ten bedrooms, the old girl could even have her own private dunny in the mansion, there was stacks of room. So what was crawling on Athol to make him want to stay in a country which was obviously going to the pack and biting its own bum?

The letter went on for twelve pages. Athol read it five times before deciding not to tell Miss Maidstone about Kezia's offer. She was too hooked up and het up over what she was to do about Fulk and the Bidwell sisters and talking of nothing else. So he wrote a quick note and said that yes, they'd decided to leave Sandspit after all and could Kezia go ahead and arrange everything and would they be allowed to stay in America for long? He wrote nothing about Enoch Fulk showing up nor about the Bidwell sisters as he didn't know how to begin explaining it. He just asked Kezia to let him know about the arrangements and left everything else unsaid, there'd be time enough if they did go to America to tell her what had happened.

When Miss Maidstone came back on her Harley from posting the letter off, fetching supplies along with a can of kero she reckoned would help put a stop to Fulk's mad plan, she'd also collected a letter from Mrs Boona Gush, which stated that all was well down at Elephant Hill, she'd arrived safely and was already hard at work dyeing sheepskins and making animals from pipe-cleaners and was so happy she wondered why she'd stayed on at Sandspit for so long. She'd found her vocation in pipe-cleaners. If there was anything at all that Athol or Miss Maidstone wanted her to do, to help them get away as well, they had only to let her know. They could put through a toll call, as there was a telephone in the house, for she was worried sick about both of them. So far there'd been no earthquakes in Elephant Hill, and only half a dozen old folk had gone down with the shingles. She herself was living on Easy Street but sleeping badly, worrying about her dear friends.

While Miss Maidstone was busy out back oiling the Harley and keeping a close eye on the temple with the telescope, Athol quickly wrote down Mrs Gush's telephone number on a piece of paper and hid it inside his shirt. Later that day, when Miss Maidstone said the coast was clear and she could get out and set her plan in motion to get rid of Fulk (she hadn't asked him to join her), Athol asked her if he could borrow the Harley-Davidson, he wanted to nick across to Babylon. Miss Maidstone had been teaching him how to use it in their spare time, back before Mrs Gush had left, and reckoned he was a natural biker and should join a club. She was so caught up in her plans she agreed as soon as he asked and didn't even query what he was up to. So he borrowed her goggles and was off down the back track past the Dairy Board factory before Miss Maidstone had even told him what she was planning to do. Athol's plan was to telephone Mrs Gush and set up a scheme to get them down to Auckland, for it would be from there they'd be leaving for America. He was dead set now on going, and making sure Miss Maidstone had no excuse to stay on. Even if they went over for a few weeks, it would get Miss Maidstone out of the Sandspit pot. Little did Athol know what was about to happen while he was out of the way.

It was two and a half hours before Athol returned to the house. Mrs Gush had kept him talking and then insisted on telephoning him back, at the Babylon post office. There was no sign of Miss Maidstone when he returned, no sign of Fulk nor the Bidwell sisters when he looked across to the temple-shack through the front door. The whole area was deserted and as quiet as a cemetery and it was already getting dark. So he pumped up the primus and fried some tomatoes and made toast and set the old rickety table up for tea, expecting Miss Maidstone to turn up at any time. He couldn't believe they'd managed to live so well in this mouldy dump of a house for so long, and although life was far different now than it'd been in Comfort Street, he and Miss Maidstone had got along just fine as if it had been natural for them to have lived the way they'd been living, amongst all the clutter and the mouldy walls and the slaters. But he'd set up his own plans now, a real future for them, and reckoned Miss Maidstone was just using Fulk's showing up as an excuse to stay put a little longer. There was no point any more, he knew that, and reckoned Miss Maidstone knew it too. She was just too scared to leave. Yet if everything worked out, then within weeks they could be shot of Sandspit Crossing for ever, leaving it to the birds and the bees and the blowflies and the wild pigs.

It'd been dark for two hours when Athol thought he'd better have a scout around along by Fulk's temple. Miss Maidstone hadn't returned. A wind had sprung up outside, rattling the wooden slats across the windows, and every sound made him leap up from the floor and peer out through the door. Outside it was almost a full moon and the sky was clear, but the air was so cold he went back inside to pull on an oilskin and check to see if there was a torch anywhere, which there wasn't.

When he reached the rear of Fulk's temple, the first thing he saw was the huge kero tin which Miss Maidstone had brought back with her from Babylon, lying on its side half-empty and up one side of the temple was a large area of burnt wood as if someone, probably Miss Maidstone, had tried to set it alight. Further along across the far side of what had been Comfort Street he could see Fulk's caravan half hidden in bush, but there were no lights on inside and no sign of the tractor. Keeping an eye on his left and right Athol ran down the Parade and headed left towards where the caravan was parked. There was no sound and no sign of life, the marquee where the Bidwell sisters were supposed to be sleeping was dark, the entrance-flap pulled completely back. When Athol ran across and stepped inside, at first he couldn't see a thing. But the tent was empty, apart from some piled-up bedding in the corner and three camp-beds lying on their sides. Athol crept out, raced across to the caravan and peered through one of the small side-windows.

He spotted Miss Maidstone straight away. She was lying hunched up in one corner on her left side, her feet and hands tied with rope and her mouth covered with something that looked like white tape.

When she saw him she started struggling and groaning and shaking her head.

It was just as he untied her, freed her mouth from the tape and she'd started telling him what had been going on – that she'd started the fire but it'd gone out as the wood was damp and Fulk had attacked her and dragged her off – when the man himself appeared in the caravan doorway. He clambered up the steps dressed in his robe with the hood pulled up over his head, swinging a large wooden crucifix covered in nails back and forth. As soon as he saw Athol he let out an almighty bellow like a stuck pig, stepping forward and hitting out with his weapon and shouting the worst obscenities Athol had ever heard, even from Norrie when he'd been drunk. Athol ducked, then shoved forward, knocking Fulk against the doorway with his shoulder, where he fell with a loud grunt. Grabbing Miss Maidstone by the arm Athol went to pull her towards the door after him but he slipped, crashing sideways against a built-in wardrobe. The door fell open with a wrenching sound, and just as Enoch Fulk had got to his feet and was about to smash the crucifix on to Athol's head, something fell out from the wardrobe, knocking Athol to the ground for a second time while he could hear Fulk shouting 'I AM JEHOVAH, OBEY ME!' and the thing that had fallen on to Athol had arms and legs and in the moonlight, which was now streaming in through the open door, it was only seconds before Miss Maidstone realized that the thing on top of Athol was the dried and mummified corpse of a man – and the man had once been Mr Reginald Wallace Ritter with all his buck-teeth still in place in his hairless skull. Miss Maidstone shrieked then with all her lung-power, falling to her knees and Athol yelled as he tried to free himself and shove the thing off his chest, and by the time they'd both managed to get to their feet and scramble outside, one of Mr Ritter's arms having fallen off before Athol had shoved the corpse as far away from him as he could, Enoch Fulk was nowhere to be seen. Miss Maidstone was unhurt but shaking like a half-axed tree and she yelled to Athol that they'd better hook their mutton and get away as fast as they could, that the would-be-if-he-could-be Jehovah-gone-haywire couldn't be far away and she knew he had a shot-gun somewhere – she was sure she'd seen one. If they could get back to the Bidwell house then one of them could bike off on the Harley to fetch the police. They had no choice now.

Hand in hand, hearts in mouths, they ran helter-skelter across the weed-covered earth, veering away from Fulk's ramshackle temple, which seemed to be glowing in the dark, racing as fast as they could manage across the flat earth still littered with blackened wood and iron, towards Anzac Avenue. Miss Maidstone's breath was rasping and after a minute she yelled out that she didn't think she could make it, it was down the chute for her, but Athol kept lifting her to her feet when she fell, propping her up and half carrying her. Just after they'd passed the temple on their left Miss Maidstone let out a screech and there was Fulk bearing down on them, having appeared from inside the temple with a shot-gun raised to his shoulder. Before they'd gone another few feet, shots were whistling past them and, as Miss Maidstone admitted later, she was convinced they were both true-blue goners and soon to be turning up in the knacker's yard, as Fulk's face when she'd glimpsed it had been ugly. With his lips pulled back and his teeth glistening from the light of the moon he was howling like a banshee and out for murder.

When they reached the Bidwell house Athol slammed the front door after them and started to barricade it with anything he could lay his hands on while Miss Maidstone stood in the hall, legs astride a large hole in the floor where the floorboards had rotted away and collapsed, crying out hysterically that they were really in the poo this time, they'd had it, but she'd fight to the bitter end, she wasn't ready to drop off the perch yet or be pushed off it, if anyone thought that they had another think coming. She didn't stop voicing off like a parrot in a half-scream and shaking from fear until Athol rushed over and held her to him in his arms and she started to sob.

Outside, beyond the barricaded door, there was a silence for a short while until they heard one, single, blood-curdling cry that seemed to go on for minutes until it suddenly stopped.

Half an hour later, when nothing more happened, they let themselves out through the back door armed with a couple of hammers. The yard was empty. The Harley-Davidson sat where Athol had left it. After kick-starting it, and once Miss Maidstone was up on the passenger seat, Athol headed out through the broken side-gate and biked flat stick along the beach track towards the Dairy Board factory before heading off to Babylon, to alert the authorities and get help. Miss Maidstone was terrified at what might have happened to the Bidwell sisters – she was afraid they would come to a sticky end if they hadn't already done so. While she was being trussed up and dumped by Fulk inside the caravan (he'd been stronger than human and bellowing that he would deal with her later), the sisters had been standing in the entrance of their tent screeching their heads off and clinging to each other, and once Fulk had left her there'd been more terrible, unearthly screaming from the sisters until they'd each fallen quiet and it'd stayed like that until Athol showed up.

The police insisted that they leave the Harley-Davidson at the Babylon station and be driven back to Sandspit in one of the two police cars. They hadn't acted all that surprised at what Miss Maidstone reported and said they believed every word, reports *had* come through that Fulk was supposed to have been in the area for some time – he'd been regarded as a dangerous criminal for a long while, years – and had deteriorated mentally after a group of determined Exclusive Brethren had taken him to court in Hamilton for fraud, but no one had thought to look for him over where Sandspit Crossing had once been, the area was thought to have been deserted after the fire. Miss Maidstone whispered to Athol while the police had filled them in that she was getting really boiled up, they were being talked at as if they were without brains instead of the other way around – these ning-nongs didn't know their bottoms from holes in the ground – it was The Ghoul all over again. The whole country was run by packs of dried up, sieve-minded rissoles. Where else should the police have been looking but Sandspit?

According to the police, Mr Enoch Fulk had been gaoled over five years ago for proven fraud but then had become ill and been transferred to the same institution that Selwyn Tuck, otherwise known as The Ghoul, had been in, and Fulk had also eventually managed to escape from that same high-security gaol for the mentally abnormal the way Tuck had escaped. By some unknown and seemingly strange turn of events Fulk had tracked down, or accidentally come across, the three Bidwell sisters, who had been running an Unmarried Mothers' Retreat not far away. Fulk was believed to have somehow overcome the sisters (by the probable use of syringing a mind-changing drug into them, and administering pills, which he was thought to have stolen from the institution before his escape) and had headed north with the drugged ladies, though there were no clues as to how he'd managed it. The three had been sighted, but the trail eventually had been lost in the bush. There were men out even now, searching for him.

Fulk had never been out of the country at all, so far as the police knew. Using money he'd hidden all over the North Island in tins buried in the earth (at which Miss Maidstone commented that great and insane minds often thought alike) – loot saved from his years as a very cunning money-grabbing preacher – he'd bought the tractor and caravan, then hired a four-wheel-drive bulldozer, but had since disappeared into thin air. The Babylon police had been sent all the known details about Fulk and had the facts on file – there were screeds of papers – and they were still studying them. Fulk had been a real hard shot in gaol, had attempted quite a few weird scams until something called paranoid schizophrenia had set in, after which he'd been transferred to the institution – his parents had also suffered from the same affliction decades before.

When Miss Maidstone asked why the heck his escape had been kept secret just as Selwyn Tuck's had been, pointing out that with all the information the authorities had had they'd still managed to bungle everything and even she could have read the clues, the police just shrugged and said the details had arrived only the day before. All they did was keep the peace and get on with the jobs in hand, they were only country sorts and were themselves forever being kept in the dark. Miss Maidstone agreed and reckoned half the country was in the Mushroom Club, in the dark being fed with scraps of poop, it was a crying disgrace.

Most of what Miss Maidstone and Athol were told was when they were being driven back to Sandspit, but before they'd even reached the outskirts Miss Maidstone had found out that the young man driving the car was a distant cousin once removed of Jack Lamb and that Jack had got back with Beryl who'd run away with Charlie Gregg the suspected Commie – Jack and Beryl were now living down in Wellington running a local milk bar and Beryl was expecting twins, she was the size of a house. Pretty soon Miss Maidstone and the young sergeant were yacking so much about past Sandspit days and about who had gone where and where so-and-so had since moved to that Athol reckoned they'd forgotten what he and Miss Maidstone had been through. Miss Maidstone even started talking about her Harley to the other sergeant, who said it was a real valuable model, as rare as hens' teeth and if Miss Maidstone wouldn't mind selling it he'd offer a real good price, he had a mate down in Wanganui who specialized in Harley-Davidsons and chrome hub-caps.

What the police, along with Miss Maidstone and Athol, discovered when they finally got back to Sandspit, struck each of them dumb for a while and was to remain with Athol for ever afterwards. By the time they arrived (the car broke down twice, Miss Maidstone finding the fault and fixing it herself) the other police car, joined by a third, both of which were fixed with spotlights on the roof, had already revealed the final chapter of the ex-Reverend Fulk's life, and the fates of Maudie, Dorothy and Bathsheba Bidwell.

The sisters' bodies were found lying in each other's arms beside a clump of manuka bush close to where Fulk had hidden his black tractor and the bulldozer. Each of them had been strangled to death with the same rope it was believed Fulk had used to haul the huge wooden cross up on to the roof of his Bethlehem temple. There'd been some attempt made to bury them, as the bodies were covered with rotting old leaves. A spade was found nearby. It was reckoned that Fulk had probably killed them after abducting Miss Maidstone, and she was certainly lucky not to have ended up the same way.

And from the base of the ten-foot-high wooden cross still pointing to the heavens on top of the jerry-built shack, Fulk's temple, hung the body of Mr Enoch-Jehovah Fulk. A hammer and nails were found on the slope of the roof. It appeared that Fulk had made an attempt to crucify himself. He'd hammered nails through both his naked feet, so it was figured out, but had then slipped, fallen backwards and somehow had smashed the back of his skull on the sharp edge of the corrugated iron, killing himself, and had hung there in death upside-down, the skirt of his robe sliding down around his head, exposing to the world that underneath it he was stark naked. Around his waist and embedded into the skin were several tightly wound strands of barbed wire. It was later that the police released the fact that they believed Fulk had been wearing the wire for some months, even before he'd escaped, as flesh had grown over parts of it and the wire had turned rusty.

After two nights staying in the Babylon Gay-Sunshine Motel, Athol and Miss Maidstone were allowed to return to the Bidwell house to pack up their belongings and be ready to move out as soon as the authorities made up their minds as to what was to be done regarding the whole area. The bodies of the Bidwell sisters and Enoch Fulk had been removed and the Bethlehem temple had been bulldozed to the ground, the same night the bodies had been discovered. Fulk's tractor, caravan and the bulldozer had been towed away and were to be kept in the Babylon Police Station yard while they were examined. For the time being, nothing was released publicly regarding the mummified corpse of Mr Ritter.

Maudie, Dorothy and Bathsheba Bidwell were to be buried together in Wellington, where they'd had distant relatives, but it was never to be revealed where Fulk's remains were to be laid to rest, after his body had been taken away and autopsied. Miss Maidstone agonized over the Bidwell sisters' deaths. She felt totally responsible, she confessed to Athol. She should have saved them somehow, she should have done more. In the end she decided she couldn't face their funeral. She and Athol sent the largest wreath they could afford, and Miss Maidstone sat on the steps of the sisters' crumbling old house and wept, the day her old friends were lowered into their final home.

The news hit the country like an atomic bomb. It was all that was talked about on the radio. Miss Maidstone, along with Athol, was photographed and interviewed by newspapers in Babylon, reporters coming from all over the country. The whole area where Sandspit Crossing had once stood had been quickly cordoned off with rope and makeshift fencing, and after some details of what had gone on had been in the newspapers for two days folk were kept well away and the area was sealed off, and would remain so for a long time, according to reports. The mind-bending drugs, pills and syringes that Enoch Fulk had used to control the tragic Bidwell sisters were examined (the caravan had been chocka), along with Reginald Ritter's preserved corpse, and slowly the truth about Mr Enoch Fulk and his vision to become the New Jehovah was revealed to the country, discussed daily on the radio and was to go down in history, along with the shingles plague – now under control – and the intermittent earthquakes, looting and arson which had caused so much hardship, as one long ugly time of New Zealand chaos. For the earthquakes, the looting and the arson, which had been dominating lives, had ceased suddenly, directly after Enoch Fulk's bungled attempt at crucifixion and his death, and Miss Maidstone wasn't the only person in the country who half believed that the events were all linked. She reckoned, she told Athol, that no one, not even herself, would ever come to within a bull's roar of finding out the real truth. There was no one on earth who had any idea why Fulk had removed Mr Ritter's corpse (unless it had been something to do with the past and they *had* known each other). He had had it – no one knew how – preserved and stuffed, and it was generally suspected that it'd been part of Fulk's truly crazed intentions to use the corpse to represent the Devil – he'd more or less admitted as much to Miss Maidstone, but she'd kept her chops closed about it when she'd talked to the police – there being no sense, she reckoned, in straining their brains even further. Though she had mentioned it to reporters.

And somehow, however truly twisted or insane it all might seem, Miss Maidstone was more than convinced after a few days that Enoch Elisha Fulk, from having first been a mere gatherer of souls, had, by some unknown and possibly supernatural force, become responsible for what was to be always regarded up and down country as the strangest crisis in New Zealand history, and she and Athol had been a part of it all.

Miss Maidstone and Athol were still in the Bidwell house a week later. No one had showed up to turf them out. All that week Athol acted as though he had a nest of biting ants up his underdungas or had fish-hooks sticking into him, as Miss Maidstone kept telling him. It was really getting up her nose – there they were, not knowing where on earth they'd be walking their chalks to from one day to the next, and on top of that she was utterly conked out from the load of public humbug they'd been exposed to, and there Athol was acting the goof, grinning like an idiot, what the heck was the matter with him, why was he rushing out front every five minutes, who was he expecting to turn up, the entire Royal Family?

But Athol just kept grinning and telling her to wait and see, she'd find out soon enough. And soon enough she did.

One morning, exactly a week after they had returned to the house from the Babylon Gay-Sunshine Motel, and after they had finally been visited by the police and been told they had two days to leave, as the house was to be demolished and the whole area bulldozed and left to return to bush, over a dozen cars, trucks and vans appeared, having come off the State Highway and been allowed to enter the still cordoned-off area. Miss Maidstone had been out front polishing the Harley with rags, calling out to Athol that the bike was the only thing, apart from some clothes and the telescope, that she wanted to take with her when they cleared out. Athol had suggested they could head off south together on the Harley, they still had money and he was sure they'd sort themselves out. Miss Maidstone had refused to discuss it. She told Athol straight that she reckoned her life was finished now. She'd be ending her days in a home full of other old oxygobblers and it'd be just her luck if one or two turned out to be Enoch Fulks. She'd be heading straight towards nightmare country when they left, she was certain of that.

As soon as she saw the parade of cars and vans and trucks heading towards her she called out to Athol that they were being invaded by a mob, and as he rushed out to join her, watching her face, she simply stared blankly with one hand shielding her eyes and the other still polishing the Harley's petrol-tank and said nothing more. Then, at the rear of the procession, appeared a beaten-up old rust-bucket of a bus, on top of which was perched a huge cardboard sign, with these words painted in bright red and gold letters: THE MAIDSTONE MAYDAY MACHINE – COME AND JOIN US! The sign was surrounded by balloons and streamers and just behind it stood a five-foot-high pine tree on an elevated base decorated with gold stars and more streamers and balloons, most of which had burst. The whole bus was decorated all over and painted sky-blue and who should be sitting in the driving seat, leaning forward and waving with one hand on the wheel, but Mrs Boona Gush, wearing a gold party hat and a lurex frock, laughing fit to bust.

Miss Maidstone put her hands up to her cheeks after crying out and stared with her mouth wide open as the entourage slowly drew closer to the house. Her face had gone bright scarlet, and as she stared she realized that every single one of the folk who were hanging out of the bus windows, or waving to her from the cars and vans and trucks, were folk she had known for decades in Sandspit, or had befriended years ago on her travels all over the North Island, folk she had written to, sent recipes, Christmas cards, birthday cards, books and Sandspit Crossing gossip but who had hardly ever bothered to reply.

As Jack and Beryl Lamb (Beryl looking hugely pregnant), Raewyn Scudder and her mum with a false foot, Mrs Dolly Mc-Arthur, on the arm of her husband Arthur, the Barker clan, Mr and Mrs Gonda, along with their son Roy, who had a young lady on his arm, as well as Mrs Gush and a sheepish-looking Charlie Gregg clambered down off the bus, followed by so many other familiar faces behind them and even more from the cars and vans, Miss Maidstone burst into floods of uncontrollable tears after letting out the loudest whoop Athol had ever heard from her lips. All the folk surrounded Miss Maidstone until she was completely lost to view and there were cries and greetings galore and Miss Maidstone's cracked voice was soon yelling out 'Eureka!' It was sheer bedlam, there beneath a cloudless blue sky in the back of beyond. And as Miss Maidstone was heard to confess later that day, it was as if all her Christmases and birthdays had arrived at once, it was one of the proudest and most joyful days of her whole life and nothing, nothing at all would ever top seeing each and every one of those happy, grinning faces appearing out of nowhere, after all the pig-island ponk she'd had to put up with over the past weeks.

When everyone had calmed down, Mrs Gush announced that they'd come to take Miss Maidstone away – they would have turned up earlier but the country was sorting itself out after the earthquakes and the roads had been hell. Many were closed and cracked to buggery. Miss Maidstone asked where were they going to take her away to, the Funny Farm or perhaps an Oxygobblers Home for the Obsolete, and Mrs Gush laughed so loudly she almost spat out her false teeth and explained that it was all in Athol's department, he was the organ-grinder, he'd telephoned her at Elephant Hill and set the balls rolling. She'd come up to Wellington, hired and decorated the bus, put an advertisement in the *New Zealand Herald* directed to all Miss Maidstone's friends everywhere and this had been the result – Athol would tell her the rest of the good news. Everyone went quiet as Athol took hold of Miss Maidstone's hands and said that he'd been in touch with Kezia and Norrie by cablegram, and that he and Miss Maidstone would be shooting through to Auckland on the bus, all the arrangements had been made for the two of them to fly out, if the earthquake damage didn't prevent it, all the way direct to America for a slap-up holiday and they'd be met at Los Angeles Airport by Kezia, Norrie and Norrie's boss Randy Delaney, in a limousine. Everything was fixed up to the last detail. All Miss Maidstone had to do was climb up on to the bus and they'd be off into the wild blue yonder.

Well, there were more tears, hugging and shouting than there'd been before and Miss Maidstone cracked on in a tearful, laughing voice that Athol was the biggest ratbaggery blighter she'd ever known. There she'd been, cleaning the Harley and thinking that after having been a rooster for years she was about to end up as a feather duster, and she couldn't have been more wrong.

After Jack Lamb and Charlie Gregg, who'd forgiven each other, had managed to haul, shove, lift and tie down the Harley on to the pram-hooks at the back of the bus, Miss Maidstone was helped on board, once they'd closed up the Bidwell house and Athol had fetched the possessions they wanted to take, leaving everything else where it lay. Within an hour the whole procession, with the decorated bus out front, was trundling down along the empty Hinemoa Parade, past the bulldozed remains of Enoch Fulk's Bethlehem temple, past the remnants of the Four Square grocery, the Majestic Picture Theatre, the Masonic Hall and turning right, along the pot-holed Rideout Road, towards the State Highway.

Half-way to Babylon, Athol (who'd been telling Raewyn Scudder's mum all about the Fulk saga, and she in turn had been showing him her brand-new artificial foot, the fourth one she'd had fitted in as many months) looked down the bus and there was Miss Maidstone sitting alone on the back seat, staring through the rear window. He knew straight away that she was weeping, as her shoulders were heaving and her head was at a strange angle. So he got up and moved forward and whispered into Mrs Gush's ear and soon Mrs Gush started singing 'She'll Be Coming Round the Mountain when She Comes' as loudly as she could manage, until the whole bus began joining in with lung-busting voices. It wasn't until they started singing a traditional Maori song, which had English words about throwing a rotten banana at your teacher, that Miss Maidstone began laughing and turned her head. She called out that she hadn't heard that ding-dong disrespectful song for donkey's years and began singing louder than anyone else and before too long she was up-standing in the aisle, belting out every New Zealand song she could remember and organizing a proper choir, with bass voices on one side and sopranos on the other.

As the bus rattled along the main street of Babylon the two front tyres suddenly had blow-outs at exactly the same time and Mrs Gush nearly crashed straight into the local petrol station but managed to swerve at the last minute, ending up in the middle of the street. Miss Maidstone herded everyone out of the bus, organized a mechanic to fix the tyres, waved down all the cars and trucks and vans following that were filled with her other friends, and headed everyone off into the Singing Tui Cafeteria on the corner, for milk shakes and sandwiches and knickerbocker glories, carrying on with the singing and remembering old rude poems from the war, and laughing non-stop.

And when Jack Lamb came hurrying in a couple of hours later to say that the tyres had been repaired, the bus was lubed and landward and they were ready for the off it was Miss Maidstone who led the way, in a conga line, looking more radiant and happy than Athol had seen her for months. Just as he was about to follow, having paid the bill after everyone had chipped in, an enormous woman wearing a pillbox hat and with features as ugly as two cows facing south, sitting in the far corner on her own reading a battered copy of The Truth, called out to the owner asking him who that awful old chook was who'd been making all the din and laughing so much, was she famous or something, she'd acted a bit like a drunken floozie, in her opinion. The owner just shrugged his shoulders and grinned and then he laughed. So Athol walked across to the woman and told her, just as Mrs Gush poked her head round the door and suggested he get his skates on, that the lady in question was none other than Miss Magdalen Maidstone of Sandspit Crossing – surely she must have read about her or seen her photograph in the newspapers? She was his best mate and the most bonzer person he'd ever known. She'd battled with a perverted preacher, a buggering butcher from Babel, a gruesome grinning ghoul and the Government, as well as some other no-hopers – all to try to save her town from dying, but now she was going off to visit America, to stay in a posh mansion which had ten bedrooms, in Hollywood, where the film stars came from.

A PETER OWEN PAPERBACK